Once Upon An Ancient Curse

An Enchanted Realms Novel

MICHELLE MILES

King Rufus
M y s
K i
Dark Wizard
D U N M E A D E
B A Y
Glenwood
Forest
E
W
Ki
Middleglen
Hollow Glen
Kingdom

Queen Seraphina
Brookdale
Vale
dom
Lighthill
Westfall
Faradill
Elven Village
Wyldwood Forest
SEA OF MARA
HANTED
ODLANDS
Clayharbor
red
Bridgefort
Feywood Kingdom
King Egbert
Ellew
ing

To the girls in red cloaks who don't run from the wolf, they hunt him.

CHAPTER 1

The wolf's howl sliced through Glenwood Forest, reverberating among the trees. Poppy crouched low, the longbow in her hand steady, the red cloak pooling around her like spilled ink in the moonlight. She no longer flinched at the sound. It was as familiar to her as the thrum of her heartbeat.

The air carried the acrid tang of wolf, sharp and bitter. It set her nerves on edge, not with fear, but with the thrill of confrontation. The Wolf King must be close—the terror of villages, the shadow in her nightmares. He had taken her parents, and tonight, she intended to meet him face-to-face.

She had trained for this moment under her grandmother's relentless eye. Hours spent mastering her longbow until the string felt like an extension of her body. But as the Wolf King's howl echoed through the forest, the burden of her purpose pressed through her. Justice, her grandmother had called it—a word that once burned with clarity. Now, it tangled with questions she couldn't silence. Could justice and vengeance ever truly be the same? And if she succeeded tonight, what part of herself would remain?

A full moon pierced the canopy above, thin beams of silver cutting through the darkness. The enchanted cloak thrummed faintly against her skin, sharpening her senses. Shadows moved differently now, their secrets laid bare. The forest's quiet breath carried whispers of predators and prey.

A twig snapped.

She raised her longbow, her breathing shallow. The silence pressed around her. Sitting a little straighter, she peered into the murky shadows, her eyes flickering from one to the next. Nothing.

Overhead, an owl hooted. The crickets chirped their nocturnal song. The wind fluttered through the treetops, swishing their leaves and clacking their branches.

Another snapping twig. She gently pulled the string taut. Straining her ears, she listened for any sounds that did not belong. The creatures of the night had gone eerily silent.

A low growl rumbled near her. She tilted her head and inhaled deeply. The pungent smell of wolf—thick and bitter—invaded her senses. A tingling sensation skipped up her spine as the hair on the back of her neck stood on end.

He was near.

She scanned the shadows until she locked on two golden eyes, watching her. Watching. Waiting. Like her. Angling her body to face him, she pointed the arrow directly at his head. The huntress was now the prey.

Poppy had a decision to make then. Release her arrow or drop her weapon? Her grandmother's voice flickered through her mind.

Never drop your guard, for he will take that moment to strike.

But he didn't appear to want to attack. In the gloom, she made out his elongated nose and the gray fur of his face, the point of his ears. His eyes missed no detail as he stared at her, and she stared back.

I know who you are.

The deep, dark rumble of a voice flickered through her mind. Her heart kicked into a wild beat. Had the beast spoken to her? And still those glowing eyes pierced her. A breath shuddered out of her as she peered down the length of her arrow.

The underbrush rustled to her left, distracting her. She glanced away from the wolf's eyes. When she turned back, he had melted back into the shadows. Gone.

To her left, the rustling sounded again. She turned toward the noise, releasing her arrow in one fluid movement. It flew into the darkness. A moment later, a *thunk* followed by a muffled oof that sounded human.

She got to her feet and hurried through the woods with her cloak flapping behind her. She found the man on the ground, her arrow lodged in his shoulder. His eyes, nothing more than black orbs, met hers, which surprised her.

Could he see her face beneath the hood, despite the magic of the cloak hiding her visage? It helped her blend into the shadows.

"Do I have you to thank for this?"

His voice was low and dangerous, each word sharp with fury as it rolled off him in waves. He grimaced, his face pinched with both pain and anger.

She crouched next to him. Blood seeped around the wound, staining his tattered shirt.

"I'm so sorry. I thought you were—"

She pressed her lips together, refusing to say more. He might have thought she was mad if she told him she thought he was a wolf. For she was certain that's what she sensed moving through the forest. His eyes met hers, those black eyes glittering with annoyance and discomfort, and her heart tripped. There was a shadow of a beard on his cheeks and chin and his hair was shaggy about his face long enough to brush his shoulders. She couldn't tell in the darkness, but he appeared to be dressed in nothing more than tatters. The shirt hung off his powerful frame, giving her a hint of his muscled chest dusted with hair beneath. His breeches were frayed, hitting him mid-calf. He wore no shoes.

"Let me help you." She held a hand out to him.

He eyed her hand with a dubious expression. "After you shot me with an arrow? I don't think so."

His words cut deep, and she flinched as guilt washed through her. "I do apologize, but you need that wound treated. My grandmother's a healer."

He frowned, his forehead wrinkling. He shook his head. "You want to take me into the village? No, thanks."

Poppy dropped her hand to her side. So, he was going to be stubborn. She changed tactics as she gave him a shrug of indifference. "Fine, then. But the wound will fester if not tended."

His mouth formed a grim line. "I suppose you're going to tell me your arrow tip was poison?"

She clutched the weapon tighter in her hand, her palm sweating. She didn't make mistakes—she was better than that—but she was startled by the rustling underbrush and sudden disappearance of the gold wolf eyes. When she started to reply, he waved her off.

"You're a huntress. I get it." He heaved a sigh and lifted a hand to her. "Help me up and take me to this grandmother of yours. But when I'm bandaged, I'm leaving."

"As you wish."

She grabbed his hand. His fingers wrapped around hers in a firm grip as she hoisted him to his feet. She stifled the gasp that wanted to erupt. He was tall, standing over her by at least a head. His shoulders were broad. His dark eyes gleamed back at her as she assessed him.

"Who are you?" she asked.

"I could ask the same of you. Why do you hide inside the cloak?"

Ah, so he was unable to see her face. The cloak protected her from unwanted attention. But it also gave her other abilities. She understood the woodland creatures—the hoot of an owl as it greeted the night, the song of the cricket's declaring their joy the sun had set. While wearing it, her senses were amplified, giving her heightened awareness to her surroundings. It also enhanced her physical abilities—she never missed a shot.

It was why she was certain when she released her arrow, she was shooting at a wolf.

She shoved off the hood, revealing her features.

There was something about his appraising scrutiny that sent chills through her. Did she imagine the spark of recognition that went through his dark, glittering eyes? He leaned toward her and inhaled a deep breath, scenting her.

A strange thing from a man with an arrow sticking out of his shoulder.

"Hm," he said. "You smell of the woods, of heather and moss."

Unsure how to respond, she motioned for him to follow. They headed through the woods back to the stone cottage she shared with her grandmother. His steps were quiet and sure-footed. More than once, she turned to make sure he was still there. As they broke through the trees, the village came into sight.

It was still deep in the night, and most were sleeping. Except for her grandmother. Poppy knew she would still be awake, sitting by the fire, knitting or darning socks for the coming winter. She often found her dozing in her chair by the fire in the morning when she returned.

The stone cottage was near the edge of the forest, surrounded by a white picket fence. It didn't take any time to reach it. She pushed open the gate and walked up the pathway to the red front door, which she pushed open. She stood aside to allow the stranger to enter. As she closed the door, he paused inside and took in their modest surroundings.

Her grandmother hobbled from the small kitchen. She had a constant ache in her left hip. With the cooler weather settling in, the limp was more pronounced. She held a towel in her hands, a questioning look furrowing her brow. Her sharp, blue eyes landed on the stranger, took in his shabby appearance as well as the arrow in his shoulder, and then looked at Poppy.

"Who's this?"

"Nana, this is..." She paused to look at him, wondering what to call him. "I accidentally shot him with an arrow."

"I see that." She motioned to the chair by the fire. "Have a seat. I'll get supplies."

Nana was not surprised to see the strange man with Poppy's arrow in his shoulder, it seemed. But then, not much surprised her.

She disappeared into her bedroom as the man walked to the wooden chair—the one Poppy frequented—and lowered himself down with a gusty sigh. The wood creaked with his weight. He stretched out his long legs. Dirt smudged along his shins and his feet. Nana would not like to see his dirty feet on her shaggy rug.

"So, that's your grandmother, eh?"

"Yes."

She placed the longbow and quiver on the floor by the door. Then she hung up her red cloak on the peg.

"She doesn't look like a grandmother."

Poppy smiled. "What should one look like, then?"

"Old," he muttered. "She walks with a limp."

"She has an ache in her hip. It becomes more difficult to manage during the winter."

"Hm," was his only reply.

He extended his hands to the fire, closing his eyes to enjoy the warmth. He appeared to have been in the forest for quite some time. How did one survive in the wild?

It was true, though. Nana wasn't the typical grandmother. Her youthful appearance belied her true age. Her hair, once the color of copper, had turned dark with a streak of silver at each temple. She left her hair long and loose. Most days she pulled it back at the nape and tied it with a leather thong. Her face held only a few wrinkles—around her mouth and the corners of her eyes—but she still had smooth, cream-colored skin. Her blue eyes were sharp and her mind sharper. She had strong hands, a strong back, and an even stronger heart. She was still one of the best with a longbow in the entire village. She taught Poppy everything she knew. She also gave her the crimson cloak when she was barely old enough to hold her own weapon.

Nana came from the bedroom then, carrying a bowl and bandages. She placed them on a nearby table and turned to him, her hands on her hips.

"What do we call you?"

He swallowed hard, his throat working, as if deciding if he should give his name or not.

"Rowan," he said, finally.

With a nod, she moved to him to assess the wound. She leaned down for a closer look at the arrow sticking out of his shoulder. She pushed aside the tattered tunic. Deft fingers probed the surrounding skin with a gentle touch.

"Well, Rowan, it doesn't look too deep. You were lucky. My granddaughter never misses." She straightened, flashed a wicked smile, and then disappeared to the kitchen.

Rowan shot her a quick look. "Are you that good?"

"Yes," she answered, strong and sure.

He lifted a dark brow under the shaggy hair that fell over his forehead. "Were you aiming for my head?"

She considered telling him yes, but then that wasn't the truth. "Actually, you weren't the target at all."

"No?"

"I was aiming at the two glowing gold eyes staring at me from the shadows, but then I heard a noise—I assume that was you—and it startled me. I reacted before thinking and released the arrow. That rarely happens."

"You mean, reacting?"

She nodded.

"So, wrong place, wrong time for me." He managed a grim smile.

"What were you doing there, anyway?" she asked, wondering if he was spying on her.

Because she was certain she hadn't seen or sensed him before, those two big, gold eyes came out to stare at her. In fact, she was certain those gold eyes belonged to the Wolf King. She missed her chance.

Nana returned then, allowing him to ignore her question. But Poppy had the sense he was there for a reason. Hunting her? Spying? Something else? She didn't know.

Her grandmother handed him a glass of amber liquid. When he gave her a quizzical look, she said, "To help dull the pain. Drink up."

He downed it in one gulp. Poppy knew what that was—Nana's prized whiskey. It would, indeed, help dull the pain. Rowan handed her back the glass. Nana set it aside, ready to work.

"This might hurt a bit," she said as she reached for the shaft.

"A bit?" He clenched his jaw as she wrapped her hand around the arrow.

She ignored him and said, "Poppy, when I have this out, hand me a bandage."

Nodding, she stepped around them and grabbed one of the gauze squares.

"I'm going to give this a yank. It should come free, but if it doesn't, I'll have to do it again," she told him.

Sweat popped out on his brow and his face drained of color. For a moment, Poppy thought he might change his mind. His gaze flickered over to her, seeking reassurance. She gave him a smile and a nod, as if to say all will be well.

Without giving him any warning, Nana grabbed the arrow as close to his shoulder as possible. She gave it a swift yank. He cried out in pain as the arrow pulled free. She held out her free hand. Poppy placed the bandage on it. Swiftly, she pressed the bandage against the wound as blood seeped from it.

"Take this arrow, Poppy, and discard it."

She did as she was asked, taking the arrow from Nana. Heading to the kitchen, Poppy broke it in half, then tossed it in the trash.

Before she left, she paused to put the kettle on for tea. As her stomach rumbled, she decided food was in order and sliced cheese, bread, and dried fruit. Placing it all on a tray, she carried it back to the living room.

Nana worked swiftly. She had already cleaned the poison from the wound and was dressing it.

"There, now. That should heal without any trouble." She stood straight, placing a hand on her back as pain flickered over her face.

She retrieved the bowl with the murky water from the table and tossed the bloody bandages in it.

"I put the kettle on, Nana." Poppy placed the tray on the low table by the worn sofa.

"You're a good girl." She grinned at her as she shuffled by and headed into the kitchen to get rid of the bloody bandages.

Rowan sat rigid in the chair, his fingers curled around the arms so tight, his knuckles leeched of color. Sweat still beaded his forehead and now rolled down the side of his face. His jaw was clenched tight.

"Whatever your grandmother used to clean the wound..." He paused, taking a deep, shuddering breath and blowing it out.

"Stung, didn't it?" Poppy moved to sit in the chair opposite him. He nodded.

"That's her special disinfectant to kill the poison. The pain will subside," she said, trying to reassure him. "You did well. I didn't hear a peep."

"I'm good with pain," he said.

"If you're hungry, you can help yourself." She motioned to the tray of food.

Rowan turned from the fire then, his eyes meeting hers and somewhere in those depths, she sensed something feral. She cocked her head to one side as a shiver went over her. A musky, wild-thing smell wafted from him, making her sit straighter in the chair.

"You...what are you?" she asked, her voice quivering.

He grinned then, showing all his teeth. Wicked teeth. Sharp teeth. Teeth that made her shrink away from him.

"I thought you'd never ask."

CHAPTER 2

Poppy stumbled from the chair, tripping over her feet as she backed away. Her eyes darted toward her longbow, her heart frantically beating.

"Don't worry. I won't hurt you." He flashed that feral smile again.

"Who are you?" she demanded, her voice strong and sure.

Why didn't she sense that about him before when she was wearing her cloak? Perhaps because she was distracted by the gold eyes or the fact he startled her, making her release her arrow.

"First, I think we should talk about who *you* are. Poppy, is it? You hunt the Wolf King."

His words skipped through her, making her heart trip. How did he know that? He said it casually as he peered at her. For a moment, she saw something wicked flicker through his eyes. Eyes the color of coal.

"Your silence is answer enough," he said.

"How do you know that?" she demanded.

Before he answered, there was the creak of a bowstring followed by Nana's frigid-as-winter's-breath voice.

"Yes, how *do* you know that? Please tell us."

Behind her, Nana held her longbow ready, sharp eyes fixed on Rowan, brow furrowed, and feet planted firmly in defense. Like her, Nana didn't miss her target. Ever. After all, she was the one who trained her.

Rowan didn't flinch at the arrow aimed at his head, sitting unmoved with a calm that seemed almost defiant.

"Everyone knows she hunts him. And you did too, at one time, didn't you, Nana?"

It was odd hearing him calling her Nana, but he had no other name for her.

"Or, perhaps I should call you...*Ruby*?" he added and punctuated it with that familiar wide smile showing all his teeth.

Poppy gasped as she spun to face her grandmother. Nana lowered her weapon and released the arrow, but kept it in her hands at the ready. She still stood in a defensive position as she stared at him, her eyes narrowed, suspicion wafting off her in waves.

How did this stranger know her grandmother's name?

"Nana?" Poppy queried.

"Enough with the games," Ruby snapped. "Don't make me regret cleaning the poison from that wound. Tell us who you are."

"I thought that obvious. The Wolf King is the terror of villages. The one who seeks his own revenge. I know enough to stay clear of him."

"Are you a wolf shifter?" she asked, determined to get to the heart of the matter. She'd sensed that feral smell about him.

"I am. I shifted before you released your arrow. Too bad for me I couldn't escape."

Poppy clenched her hands into fists. "I *did* smell you. I wasn't wrong about that."

"No, you weren't. The two glowing golden eyes you saw in the shadows was the Wolf King. He would have pounced if I hadn't distracted you."

"You meant to intervene, then?" she asked.

He merely nodded.

Poppy glanced back at her grandmother, who relaxed but continued to clutch the longbow in her hand. There was some long forgotten, deep knowledge in her eyes that maybe she didn't want to share.

"The cloak would have protected me," she said.

She walked to the table with the food and picked up a piece of bread. In the kitchen, the kettle whistled, announcing it had finally come to a boil.

"Are you sure about that?" he asked.

His response sent a niggling of doubt through her. Her grandmother told her all her life the cloak would protect her from the dangers in the forest. But was it true? She cast a questioning look her way, but Nana's face remained impassive.

"You didn't answer the question how you knew she was hunting the Wolf King," Nana said, her words sharp.

A ghost of a smile flickered over his face. "Everyone knows she's hunting him. You did, too, at one time. Didn't you, Ruby?"

The use of her grandmother's given name was disconcerting. Rowan knew a lot more than he let on. That bothered her. She shifted from one foot to the other, still holding the piece of bread she had yet to eat. Her grandmother's face remained stoic.

"I did. Once. That was a long time ago."

This was information Poppy never had. Shock hit her like a punch in the gut.

"Nana?"

It was all she managed to say. Questions still formed in her mind as she tried to understand.

"The Wolf King killed innocents," she said, her glittering, hard eyes still on Rowan. "Including my daughter- and son-in-law."

"So, you retaliated," Rowan said casually. As if he knew this information already.

Poppy's head swiveled between the two of them as she waited for Nana's reply.

"I had no other choice. I wanted him to pay for what he did. He took my only daughter from me. I wanted him dead."

Of course, she knew about the death of her parents. Nana shared the story with her many times. The Wolf King earned his name because he was one of the largest dire wolves ever seen. He attacked their village during their annual harvest festival. But what she didn't know was that her grandmother took to the forest to hunt him down and destroy him.

"That's why you trained me, isn't it?" Poppy's weak voice punched through the thick silence.

Nana turned to her, her eyes softening. She took a step toward her, but Poppy moved away.

"You must understand, dearest, I trained you so you could protect yourself if he ever found us again."

But Poppy didn't believe her. "You trained me to be your weapon—to finish what you started."

Guilt flashed over her face before she managed to conceal it. That flicker of guilt was all Poppy needed. It was a confirmation, a tiny crack in her grandmother's defenses that exposed the truth beneath years of silence. But Poppy knew she was right. What else had her grandmother lied to her about?

"Well, the Wolf King *has* found you again," Rowan said. "Now...what are you going to do about?"

Poppy flung the piece of bread onto the tray. "I'm not doing anything about it. And neither are you, Nana. I need some air."

Then she stormed to the door, flung it open, and stepped out. She punctuated her anger by slamming the door. She stood there in the early morning hours, shivering. She wished she had thought to grab her cloak. Instead, she clutched her elbows and took a step away from the door, heading to the woods.

At the gate, she paused and stared into the deep shadows of the world beyond their small village. They lived in the Hollow Glen Kingdom, in the realm of the Enchanted Woodlands. The forest ahead of her was the Glenwood Forest. The realm held every manner of creature—from elves to sprites to unicorns. There was magic within the trees, the flora, the fauna. After all, the realm wasn't called *enchanted* for no reason.

And now a massive, dangerous, dire wolf resided within the trees.

She'd grown up within the towering oak trees, learning to hunt and shoot. She had never feared the forest or the magic within it. Now, she dreaded what lurked within the murky mist of day and the sinister shadows of night.

Behind her, she heard the door open and close. She assumed her grandmother came out to join her.

"You needn't lecture me about my behavior. I know it was rude to storm out," she said without turning around.

"It wasn't rude."

It was Rowan who answered. Poppy spun to face him, her heart kicking into a rapid beat. He walked down the stone path carrying her red cloak. He seemed unfazed by the cool wind stirring his long hair.

"Oh, I thought you were my grandmother."

He draped the cloak over her shoulders as he joined her. She was grateful for it and wrapped it tight around her. As he paused next to her, he peered into the gloom of the forest.

"You know, there is a legend the Wolf King was once a man."

She tipped her head to the side. "I've heard no such legend."

Rowan was undeterred by her interruption. "Long ago, in a time of great magic, there was a guardian of an ancient power that held the balance of our world. Damon was his name. His duty was his life. He pledged an oath to protect it, an oath that could not be broken, not even for love."

Poppy wasn't sure where he was going with this. A shudder went through her. Rowan peered straight ahead at the misty shadows of dawn.

"Damon, though, fell in love with a woman he knew he could never have. A fierce love doomed from the start because his duty required his unwavering loyalty. The village his lover lived in sat atop a ley line of great power."

Her brows pulled together in question. "Why are you telling me this?"

"Shh. I'm getting to that." A ghost of a smile flickered over his face.

In that instance, Poppy did not deny his good looks or his charm. He was weaving a spellbinding story.

"His lover discovered the truth of the ley lines—that the magic would erupt from the earth during the time of the super blue moon. This terrible destruction would bring ruination to her people. Desperate to protect the village, she made a heartbreaking choice. She betrayed Damon. But when she did, she invoked an ancient curse that turned him into the Wolf King, a dire wolf bound by the magic he swore to protect."

His voice grew soft with the weight of the story, as if it deeply affected him. He drew in a long breath and released it slowly. She waited, silent, for him to continue.

"Rage and sorrow consumed him in his cursed form. He attacked the village, taking the lives of many innocents. His lover, driven by her own grief and guilt, hunted him. But he found her first. She was grievously wounded and should have died. But she didn't. She survived."

As he finished the story, the leaves rustled in the trees on the wind, giving it an ominous feel. Her mouth went dry as she stared into the shadows leaking from the trees, standing like sentries, guarding all within the woodlands.

She felt, deep down, he told her this story for a reason. Understanding punched through her, making her heart race and her pulse skip.

"His lover...who was she?" Poppy asked.

"I cannot say."

Frustration edged through her. "You cannot or you will not?"

He said nothing, merely continued to stare into the forest. Dew glistened on the blades of grass in the faint morning light. Cold fear skipped through her, tingling the back of her neck and making the hairs on her arms stand on end. She suspected she knew who Damon's lover was, and it cut her deep.

Rowan turned to her suddenly, reaching for her, gripping her upper arms. "There's more. It won't be easy for you to hear."

His eyes searched hers with a hidden desperation and underlying empathy. It tugged at her.

"What is it? Tell me."

"This enchanted cloak you wear..." He brushed his hand down her arm. "It's tied to the ancient power and holds the key to the curse."

His expression hardened then. "The Wolf King is driven by vengeance, but buried beneath that is a man tormented by his love for a woman who betrayed him. That betrayal defined his fate."

"But...curses can be broken, can't they?"

He nodded slowly. "It can. To break it, we must face him and find a way to restore balance."

"We? Are we a team now?"

"You need me," he said.

She chewed on her lower lip. She had never needed anyone. Now, this man, this wolf shifter, thrust himself into her life while out there, another man cursed to be a dire wolf, hunted her. Did he seek her for a reason? Did he know her? And if so, why? How?

"Who was his lover, Rowen?"

Silence stretched between them. "I think you know."

She didn't want to admit it, even to herself. But the only answer was that her grandmother, Ruby, was Damon's lover. *She* had betrayed him. *She* had enacted the curse in a desperate attempt to protect the village. And yet, her parents had died anyway.

And her grandmother was the one to hunt him down, intent on destroying him. He, in turn, attacked her, giving her that limp. Injuring her. A daily reminder of all that happened to her in a previous life. A life Poppy never knew about.

Now, she wondered if her vengeance was misguided by her grandmother. Perhaps it was her grandmother who wanted vengeance upon the Wolf King. Perhaps her grandmother cast this Wolf King in an evil light to finally do away with him.

"Poppy, I can help you track the Wolf King."

She clutched her elbows again as the fear pounded through her. Nana never told her this. It seemed Nana never told her a lot of things. She spun toward the door of the cottage and hurried up the path.

He called, "Where are you going?"

"To get some answers."

CHAPTER 3

T he door slammed behind her. She stood, rigid, her hands shaking as fury pumped through her. Nana was in the kitchen, clanking dishes. The smell of freshly brewed tea wafted through the small cottage. Bergamot and lemon. She charged into the kitchen.

Nana turned, her face impassive. As if she were not surprised to see her standing there with the anger pounding through her.

"Did you lie to me?" Poppy's voice quivered, barely above a whisper.

"I never lied to you, dearest child. Everything I did was to protect you." She picked up the tea kettle and poured the tawny liquid into a porcelain cup.

"Including hunting down the dire wolf yourself?"

She poured a second cup. "What did he tell you?"

She asked it so casually it was as though she was unconcerned with what Rowan told her. Maybe she was. Maybe she had come to the realization she could no longer lie to Poppy, that she had to come clean with whatever truth she kept hidden all these years.

"He told me you hunted him. That you were attacked by him. That's why you have trouble with your hip, isn't it?"

"Come, sit, and have some tea, dear." She gestured to the scarred wooden table and creaky chairs.

But Poppy didn't want tea, and she didn't want to sit. She wanted answers. "Nana—"

"Sit."

Her expression was stern and unyielding. She set the tea tray on the table and sat at its head, waiting for Poppy to join her. With some reluctance, she pulled out the chair next to Nana, the legs scraping along the wooden floor, and lowered herself into it.

Nana brought one of the porcelain cups to her, then dropped in a lump of sugar. She stirred, her motions unhurried. Then she reached for the second cup and placed it in front of Poppy. The sharp scent of bergamot curled in the steam, its warmth brushing her face like an old comfort.

"We have not always lived in his village," Nana said, her tone cold and soft.

Poppy could not remember a time when she lived anywhere else. "Yes, we have."

"No." She shook her head so hard, a lock of hair fell over her shoulder. She tucked it behind her ear. Irritation wafted off her in waves. "I had hoped I would never have to tell you this story."

Poppy wrapped her cold hands around the porcelain tea cup relishing the warmth of the brew inside. She waited, watching her grandmother intently as she searched for the right words. Nana's hands shook. It occurred to Poppy, then, her grandmother was nervous and maybe a little afraid to tell her whatever truth was hidden deep within her. She reached for her, placed a hand on her arm and gave a gentle squeeze.

"It's all right, Nana. Whatever it is, you can tell me."

She offered a faint smile. "The day your parents died was deceptively beautiful—a cool spring morning with a breathtakingly blue sky. It was harvest time, and they were out picking radishes and carrots. It was early, you see, not long after dawn. I was at the local market buying necessities. Flour, sugar, eggs, and the like.

"When I returned later that morning, it was like walking into death. The smell of it was pungent on the air. And something else. A strong, musky animal odor."

She paused to take a sip of her tea, her hands still shaking. Poppy remained silent as she waited for her to continue.

"No one expected it to happen. The dire wolf melted out of the early morning dawn, it seemed. He attacked without warning. He killed your parents and several others before he was chased away by the other villagers. I tried to get the leaders to go after him, to hunt him down and kill him, but they refused. They were too afraid of the dire wolf. He was huge, you see. Standing almost as tall as a man with gray fur and bright gold eyes."

Poppy sucked in a breath. *Gold eyes* like the ones peering at her from the shadows that morning.

"We were ordered to stay in our homes. But I was determined to rid our lives of this menace. You were a babe at the time. I left you in the care of my neighbor. I went in search of the wolf. I was not as skilled as I am now. He found me first. He swiped me with his massive paw. I carry the scars to this day. The only thing that protected me was the red cloak."

Horror gripped her as she imagined how close her grandmother had come to death, leaving her an orphan. Another pause as she took another sip of her tea. She placed the delicate cup in the saucer.

"After I healed, I was asked to leave the village. They didn't want me there anymore. They were afraid the Wolf King would return to finish what he started. I packed up and moved here, to Middleglen."

"Why have you never told me this before?" Poppy demanded.

"Because I was afraid of the truth," she said. "Afraid if you knew the truth, it would set you on a path you could never turn away from. I trained you to protect you, to ensure you'd be ready if the Wolf King returned."

"Don't you mean you trained me in the hopes I would exact *your* revenge for killing my parents? For injuring you? All my life, you told me stories of this Wolf King, that he was dangerous. That he killed with malice."

"He did. He *does*," she said, her voice raw with emotion.

"Tell me the truth, Nana. He came after you because you betrayed him, cursing him."

Her eyes widened, then guilt collapsed her face. "Told you, he did. This Rowan."

"He told me of the legend of a cursed man, sworn to be a guardian of an ancient magic."

"That's true. And it would have destroyed the village. The ancient prophecy foretold a guardian harnessing the power beneath the village to maintain the balance of the world. I couldn't allow that to happen."

"So, you betrayed him."

"I wanted to protect the village from this devastating destruction. His guardianship was a secret few knew. I was one of them. I exposed that secret. When he came to claim the power of the ley lines, the leaders revolted. They drove him out. He was unable to fulfill the prophecy."

"And at a terrible cost," Poppy added.

"The magic from the ley lines erupted without anyone to control it. As the curse was completed, the ley line power fused with the cloak. *My* red cloak. Now yours."

"It should have been his power, then," Poppy said. "Not yours or mine."

"I didn't choose that to happen," Nana said, sounding defensive. "It happened as a consequence of the curse—magic drawn to magic—and to maintain balance. And it saved the village from being destroyed."

Poppy thought about this for a long moment. If all this was true, didn't it make sense that her red cloak was the key? Maybe there was a way to break the curse.

"The Wolf King attacked other villages," Poppy pointed out. "It wasn't some random act of violence, was it? He's looking for you."

"No." Nana shook her head. "He's looking for the red cloak. That's why he attacked the village when you were a babe."

The Wolf King found the red cloak—on her. Her parents died because of Nana's defiance and betrayal.

Poppy's chest tightened as a wave of betrayal swept over her. Nana's actions, meant to protect, had instead cast a shadow over her life—a shadow she'd unknowingly carried. She dropped her cup and pushed from the table. She turned away from Nana. What was she supposed to do now?

"Did you plan this?" Poppy asked.

"Gods, no," she said on a gasp. "I gave you the red cloak for protection."

Poppy spun to face her, her ire rising. "And why did you train me from the moment I was old enough to hold a longbow?"

Nana pressed her lips together in a thin, straight line. And for a moment, guilt flickered through her eyes.

"I trained you so you would know how to defend yourself."

"Sending me out every night to hunt the Wolf King is *not defending myself.*" Her voice hitched as emotion clotted her throat. "Why don't you admit it, Nana? You trained me, you gave me the red cloak, you told me stories of the Wolf King attacking villages and killing people—my parents!—because you hoped I would pick up where you left off. Isn't that right?"

Even as the words left her mouth, Poppy hated the bitter edge in her voice, but she couldn't suppress it. The truth had festered too long.

Nana rose without a word, her face a mask. She left the kitchen, retreating to her bedroom in silence. The click of the door was the only sound in the small cottage.

Poppy made an impulsive decision. She headed to the front door, snatched up her longbow and quiver, and stormed out.

Rowan still stood on the footpath at the gate. He turned as she stepped outside, his eyes steady and unreadable, like he'd been waiting for her to return. She halted in front of him.

"Does the offer to help me track the Wolf King still stand?" she asked.

"It does."

"Good. Then I'd like to take you up on it. When do we start?"

CHAPTER 4

The morning sun rose higher in the sky, and, for the first time, Poppy noticed shimmering silver strands in Rowan's dark, shaggy hair. Though his eyes were dark, when the light hit them, it was as though she could see right into the depths of them. Right to his soul. The soul of the man he was, not the wolf.

In that moment, she sensed all she needed to know about him. He was a man who wanted nothing more than to live a normal life. He wanted a wife, children, a home. But he was tormented by his shifter abilities. He wanted to be accepted for who and what he was, not feared.

He unwittingly caused fear in those who loved him most. His village treated him as a pariah, until, at long last, they cast him out. Out of fear and a deep desperation to safeguard their people. He left, cursed himself to roam the wilderness alone as a man and a wolf.

She knew all of this when she looked into his eyes because the magic of the cloak buzzed through her veins. The magic revealed to her the world around her. She never expected it to reveal so much about the man before her.

"We have much to prepare before we embark on this quest," he said, unaware she saw deep into his soul. "You should rest."

She stared at the stone cottage, the place she had always called home. Now it felt more like a cage, holding truths she couldn't unsee. The last thing she wanted to do was go back inside to face her once again. Her anger simmered beneath the surface, ready to boil over.

"We will leave together after night falls," he continued.

She peered at the ruby front door.

"You don't want to go back inside," Rowan said, matter-of-factly.

"No."

"I take it you got your answers. Answers you didn't like."

"Everything you told me was true. But there is more you don't know."

"Like?"

"My red cloak...the magic is tied to the magic of the Wolf King."

He was silent for a long moment as he contemplated this. "That's a twist I didn't expect."

"Nor I."

"What does it mean? That your cloak is tied to the magic?" he asked.

She told him the story as Nana related it to her. That when the curse was enacted, the magic from the ley lines had to go somewhere to maintain the balance. All these years, the magical balance of the world was embedded within the fibers of her cloak.

"If we break the curse, will the magic in the cloak no longer work?" he asked.

"That's my assumption."

The thought of losing her cloak, though, was painful. She did not know one day without it. It had been a part of her and her family for decades. But if she had to give it up, she would.

"We need to find the Wolf King."

"We do and we will, but we should wait until night fall. And I need to find some proper clothing. I can't be traipsing about the forest in...well, this." He indicated his tattered clothes and his bare feet.

He had a point. Finally, she nodded with agreement. "Then we meet back here at dusk."

When they parted ways, she went back inside the stone cottage and straight to the loft where her bedroom was. Nana's bedroom door was closed, a silent barrier between them. She had nothing else to say to her.

She climbed the stairs to the loft, kicked off her boots, and placed the cloak across the back of her dressing table chair. She changed into her nightdress, climbed under the covers, and was asleep minutes later.

She had a fitful sleep, as much as she tried to rest. When the sun dipped closer to the horizon in the late afternoon, she rose, dressed and gathered her cloak. Downstairs, Nana was in the kitchen. A simmering pot was on the stove, giving off its aromatic scent of rich meat and vegetables. Rabbit stew. Bergamot and lemon hung in the air indicating she had also brewed a pot of tea.

She hung her cloak up at the door, then headed to the kitchen. When she entered, Poppy halted. Nana was at the stove, stirring the stew. The teapot and cups were in the center of the table along with bread bowls. Three of them. As if she expected company.

"Have a seat. Supper's ready," Nana said without turning.

"Nana—"

"I know what your plan is. You don't have to tell me."

A knock sounded on the door. Poppy froze as she stared at her grandmother. Silence hung thickly between them. Another knock.

"You should get that," Nana said.

Poppy strode to the front door, whipping it open. Rowan stood on the other side looking much different than he had that morning. His shaggy hair was combed and neatly tied at the nape of his neck with a leather thong—she hadn't realized his hair was so long. He wore a tunic with lace ties at the throat, a padded leather vest, a hooded cloak, black pants, and well-worn black boots that indicated a rough, nomadic life. A sheath for a dagger rested on one hip. The faint scent of rose water clung to him, soft and unexpected against the sharp, feral presence she associated with him.

A sheepish look flickered over his face, as though he was hesitant to step foot inside the cottage. Poppy suspected there must have been a conversation she wasn't privy to between her grandmother and Rowan.

"Don't stand there all day. You're letting the chill in," she called from the kitchen. "Come eat."

"Your, ah, grandmother invited me," he said.

Poppy lifted a brow, unsure how to respond. She stepped aside and allowed him to enter, then followed him to the kitchen.

"Would either of you care to explain what's going on here?" Poppy said.

"I asked Rowen to come," Nana said. "You should both have a decent meal before you go on this wild hunt of yours."

She brought the stew from the stove, then ladled a heaping spoonful into each bread bowl. Then she poured steaming tea into each cup. When neither of them moved from the doorway, she waved to the table.

"Sit. Eat."

Rowan kept his eyes downcast as he moved into the small kitchen and took one of the seats. The chair scratched along the wood floor as he pulled it out.

"Poppy, where are your manners? Take the man's cloak."

"That's not necessary." He shrugged it off and draped it over the back of the chair, then sat.

Poppy looked between the two of them. Nana was busy at the stove. Rowan stuck his spoon into the stew and started to eat. She didn't deny the rumble of her stomach, but she had questions.

"What is going on?" she asked.

"After you went to bed, I went to find Rowan," Nana said without turning from the stove. She was stirring something in a large black pot. Steam rose from whatever was inside.

"Why?" Poppy demanded.

"Because I wanted to make sure he was going to keep you safe." She dropped the spoon and turned to face her. "You're all I have left, Poppy."

The ice in her heart melted a little hearing that. She set aside the anger simmering under the surface to see it from her grandmother's point of view. Hunting down the Wolf King—for real this time—must be terrifying for her. She'd lost her daughter and her son-in-law to the vicious animal and now, Poppy was going headlong into dangerous territory.

Rowan froze with his spoon hovering over the bowl. His eyes—those deep, dark, beautiful eyes—were wide with a mixture of fear and concern. Poppy understood then, he didn't want to come between her and her grandmother.

"I vowed I would make sure no harm would come to you. I promised I would bring you home safe."

As he said it, his eyes met hers and somewhere deep within her she knew without a doubt he would make good on that vow. Finally, she pulled the chair out and sat.

"And then I invited him to supper," Nana said in a cheerful voice as if they weren't about to go on a dangerous quest.

She continued to stir her black pot. Something sweet smelling wafted from it as steam rose. She turned off the burner and set down the spoon, then grabbed a small vial. With a careful hand, she poured the tawny liquid from the pot into the vial, capped it with a cork, and then placed it beside Poppy.

"What's that?"

"It's a tincture." Nana sat at the third spot and picked up her spoon. "In case you get injured, drink it. It will help heal you."

Poppy started to object but instead said, "Thank you, Nana."

"Now, eat up, both of you. You have a long night ahead."

Chapter 5

Once they finished eating, Nana packed a knapsack with bread, cheese, and dried fruit and gave them a waterskin—in addition to the healing tincture. Poppy pulled on her red cloak, slung her quiver of arrows over her shoulder, and grabbed her longbow. She pocketed the small vial with the healing tincture. Rowan took charge of the food and waterskin. As he followed her to the door, he wrapped his cloak around his shoulders and pulled up the hood.

They'd decided to move under the cloak of darkness, saving their strength for daylight hours. The Wolf King, Rowan said, was a nocturnal creature.

Nana trailed behind him as they headed to the door. Though she tried to mask her worry and concern with her impassive expression, Poppy saw it anyway.

"When will you return?" Nana asked.

"When we find what we're looking for," Poppy said.

Or, she thought, when they accomplish what they'd set out to do. Kill the Wolf King. Or, mayhap, release him from his curse.

There was an awkward beat of silence as Poppy pulled open the door to the stone cottage and stepped out. Rowan slipped by her into the gloaming and waited for her on the stone pathway near the gate while she said her farewells.

"Will you kill him?" The question was tentative.

"I don't know," Poppy answered truthfully.

It was a question she asked herself. If she killed him, would the curse break? And if he died, what happened to the wild, unfettered magic in her cloak? Would it then return to the ley lines in her home village? Or would it unleash mayhem into the world?

"I understand." Her grandmother's hand on her arm was steady, but the tremble in her voice betrayed her fear. "Come home safe." The words sounded like a plea—and an apology.

Poppy nodded, unable to meet her grandmother's eyes. Heavy unspoken expectations pressed against her back as she turned away, the silent plea lingering in the air—*finish what I couldn't*. But was that the right thing to do? She joined Rowan and, together, they walked out the gate into the night. Into the unknown.

Rowan moved ahead, his long strides cutting through the darkness with a certainty she envied. He slung the knapsack with the food over one shoulder. Poppy followed, each holding their silence. She couldn't decide if the silence was comforting or unnerving. As he walked ahead, his movements were quiet and assured, like he belonged to the shadows that surrounded them. She wished she could say the same for herself.

Why did he want to track the Wolf King? Why was he so ready to help and trust her? What did he have to gain?

He paused there to inhale the air. Poppy inhaled, too, and scented the damp heather and the sharp, sweet scent of the bracken. She pulled up her hood, letting it conceal her face as she closed her eyes and tuned into her surroundings.

As even-fall continued, she heard the last twitter of birds as they settled in for the night, the crickets chirping as they emerged for their nocturnal chorus, the rustle of creatures foraging for their evening meal. Somewhere deep in the forest, she heard the faint howl of a wolf.

She opened her eyes.

"He's here."

"He's close," Rowan agreed. "But he doesn't want to be found. He wants to hunt. We must be cautious."

She understood that to mean he wanted to hunt *her*. He wanted to find her again. What would happen when or if he did? Would he attack her like he did her grandmother?

They picked their way through what was once a trail but now overgrown. Rowan pushed aside the overhanging leaves and branches, holding them aside long enough for her to follow.

"Do you know where you're going?" she asked.

"I have an idea where his lair is."

"Where is it?"

"In the far reaches of the forest." He paused, then turned to her. "It will be a long, dangerous trek. I hope you're ready for that."

She lifted her chin a little higher and gripped her longbow a little tighter. "I'm ready for anything."

"Good."

He resumed his walk through the dense foliage, his feet silent on the ground. She marveled at that. Almost as though he were in some type of stealth mode. As she watched him, she admired the way he walked with a sort of fluid, graceful motion. He belonged here in the forest.

In the distance, a wolf howled giving them both pause. He cast a glance backward at her.

"The Wolf King?" she asked.

"No."

The wolf howled again.

"My pack." His voice was low, rough, and tinged with something primal. He pushed onward through the dense thicket, branches snapping underfoot like the ticking of a clock. "They're calling to me."

Her pulse stuttered, then pounded in her throat. The hair on her arms stood on end, an instinctive warning she couldn't ignore.

"They know I'm out here, somewhere. They want me to return to the pack."

A chill swept over her skin, tightening her chest. Her breath hitched, shallow and fast, as though her lungs couldn't draw in enough air.

But he couldn't return, because he was in human form, which made her wonder *how* he was still in human form. She contemplated this for a long, silent moment as they continued their trek.

"Go ahead. Ask me," he said, pushing aside branches.

"Ask you what?" Despite the question, she thought she understood what he meant.

"You want to know why I'm not with them. Why I'm still in human form."

"Well... yes."

"I agreed to help you," he said. "I can't do it in wolf form."

"No, but—"

"I drank a tincture to suppress my shifting abilities. Your grandmother gave it to me."

That made her halt. "She what?"

But Rowan continued to walk. "She knew, as I did, if I turned, I would be unable to protect you."

"I can protect myself." She sounded indignant even to her own ears. And how dare her grandmother interfere?

"Not from the Wolf King. He's dangerous."

She pushed onward, past him and into the deepening twilight. "I'm not afraid of him."

His booted feet crunched on the bracken behind her. It was the first time she'd noticed he actually made a sound when he moved.

"You should be. He is not to be taken lightly."

She spun to face him, her eyes blazing like embers catching fire. "Don't you think I know that?" Her voice cracked, raw with suppressed grief and fury. "I know better than anyone. He killed my parents."

The words tore out of her, leaving her chest heaving. Her grip on the longbow tightened until her knuckles ached, her nails biting into her palm. Pain shot up her arm, but she didn't let go. She couldn't. It was the only thing grounding her in the maelstrom of her rage.

Anger rippled through her body in waves, hot and consuming, until it felt like it might boil over and spill from her in a scream. Her jaw ached from clenching it so hard, her teeth grinding as though she could bite down on the memory and make it disappear.

The surrounding shadows seemed to deepen, the oppressive weight of the night pressing down on her. She barely registered him stepping closer until his hand brushed her arm.

"Don't—"

Her voice faltered as his touch steadied her, cool and grounding like a balm against a searing wound. Her body betrayed her anger, her rigid muscles slackening under his steady presence.

For a moment, she hated the way his gentleness unraveled her defenses. The fury ebbed, leaving her hollow, and in its place came the sharp ache of loss that never truly left.

"I meant no offence. I've seen what he can do. I promised your grandmother I would protect you. I never go back on a promise."

She drew a breath, slow and deliberate, then exhaled and unclenched her jaw. "Then promise *me* something, Rowan."

"Of course."

"Promise me when it comes time to confront him, you allow me to do it."

Even in the darkness, she saw the concern flicker through his dark gaze. He didn't want the Wolf King dead. Perhaps he merely wanted to break the curse and return him to what he once was—a man. But Poppy could not allow him to terrorize this earth one more day.

He nodded. "You have my solemn word."

CHAPTER 6

Poppy wasn't sure she was actually going to kill the Wolf King. Her life had certainly led her to that ultimate moment, but after learning so much about the past and her grandmother's involvement in it, she was not so sure anymore.

The thought of breaking the curse gnawed at her, persistent and unrelenting. She didn't know how to do it, but the idea rooted in her mind, refusing to let go. Would this Wolf King then revert to the man he once was with his memories intact? She didn't know. And if he didn't remember what he'd done as a fierce dire wolf, was it right to take his life?

There was the possibility he *would* remember and then she had to decide on her next actions.

Another distant howl broke the silence, low and mournful. It carried an ache that sent a shiver up her spine—an ache that sounded like it missed him. Was he their leader? Was that why they continued to howl?

A low growl nearby got both their attentions. He halted, as did she, and glanced back at her. Poppy closed her eyes and tuned into her senses using the red cloak. She heard the skitter of creatures under the brush as they hurried to move away from whatever threat loomed. The crickets stopped chirping. The owl flew away, his massive wings flapping with a thump.

All the night creatures had gone eerily silent.

Opening her eyes, she met Rowan's dark orbs. Deep within them, she saw concern mixed with a little fear.

Poppy reached behind her and drew an arrow from her quiver. As she slid it against her longbow, ready to pull the string taut, he shook his head. He pressed a finger against his lips, indicating silence.

The animal snarl sounded again.

Poppy sensed through the enchanted fibers they were being watched. Ahead of her, the shapes of trees, leaves, fallen logs, and other flora were bathed in inky blackness. With the power of the cloak, though, she saw them clearly.

As well as the two glowing gold eyes peering at her shrouded by darkness. She remained still as they stared at each other.

He drew her in, deeper and deeper. And suddenly an image burst through her mind. An image of the man he once was chopping wood outside a cabin. He paused, smiling at someone who caught his attention. He was handsome, then. Tall, with eyes the color of amber, and long pale blond hair pulled back at the nape tied with a leather thong. His tunic was sweat dampened.

His smile faded suddenly as he peered at someone. But she heard the man's voice flickering through her mind.

The time has come, Damon. The lines are breaking. The magic will rise. You will take your place as guardian.

Damon shook his head and said something back to the man.

Aye, you will. You swore an oath. You will keep that oath.

His face was lined with regret. He said something again.

Then you will face the consequences.

The vision faded. Rowan shouted her name.

She realized with some horror she was flat on her back looking up at the dire wolf, his massive paw pressing on her chest as he stood over her showing all his teeth. His black pupils expanded, swallowing the gold irises. His feral smell wafted over her. A deep rumble resonated from his massive chest.

But she was not afraid.

She had the magic of the cloak to protect her.

You stole what is mine. I want it back.

The deep, gravel voice exploded through her mind. She heard it for what it was—a warning.

Then he was gone in a flash. Rowan's face creased with worry as he appeared in her line of vision.

"Are you all right?"

"What happened?" she asked as she struggled to sit up.

Rowan crouched next to her, helping her. Her chest throbbed where the dire wolf stood. She rubbed at it, trying to make the pain go away.

"You were standing there one minute, then the next the wolf leapt and landed on you. I shouted your name but the whole thing only lasted a moment. Then he was gone."

In that moment, she had witnessed something from his past through the magic of the cloak.

"Poppy..." His voice trembled on her name. "Your cloak..."

She was so distracted by the pain in her chest, she hadn't realized her cloak was shimmering in the darkness. As though the magic had come alive within the fibers.

"What's happening to it?" She tried to keep her voice even, but there was distinct fear flickering through her. The cloak had never done that before.

"Maybe because the Wolf King was so close it triggered the magic in the cloak."

She met his eyes. "I heard his voice in my head. He said I stole something from him, and he wants it back."

Or else.

"The cloak," he said.

"Yes," she agreed.

He held a hand down to her. She took it as he helped her up to her feet.

"We better find some shelter for the night and rethink our plan," he said.

She nodded agreement, though they hadn't really discussed a plan. She merely followed him into the woods. It was hard to shake the fear skipping through her. Her arms tightened around herself, a futile attempt to shield against the chill—not from the forest, but from the uncertainty troubling her. When Rowan handed back her weapon, his steady presence both reassured and unnerved her. She slipped it over her shoulder.

"There's an old cottage not far from here," he said.

Curiosity itched at her tongue—how did he know about the old cottage? Of course, he'd know about the cottage. He was a shifter. He lived in and roamed these woods.

It was a short walk to the dilapidated building which wasn't much more than a roof and four walls. Rowan kicked open the door. It flung inward revealing the one-room cottage. If it could even be called that. The dirt floor was smooth and cool. But it would be enough to give them shelter for the night.

And then what? Resume their trek in the morning?

She followed him inside to look around. "Not much to look at."

"I'll get some firewood. We can at least have a fire for the night."

He disappeared out the door again, leaving her alone. She slid her weapons off and placed them on the floor, then sat next to them. It was dark and chilly. She pulled her cloak tighter around her frame. The fibers had finally stopped shimmering. But she was curious about it. Maybe Rowan was right in that the magic in it sensed the Wolf King.

As she contemplated this, she pulled out her waterskin and took a drink.

If Damon was to be a guardian of the magic that had seeped from the ley lines, then...

Her thoughts trailed away when Rowan returned. He quickly set about building a fire. He pulled matches from his pocket, striking one on the tinder box and lighting the dried leaves to get it started. It wasn't long before it crackled to life, throwing a warming glow around their surroundings.

"Rowan, if Damon was supposed to be the guardian of the magic from the ley lines and that magic went into my cloak..." She paused, trying to decide how to ask the question forming in her mind.

He stopped what he was doing to look at her over the flickering flames. "You have a theory?"

"What if my cloak is the key to breaking the curse?" There. She'd said it.

His dark brows drew together in question.

She told him, then, of the vision she had with the dire wolf—the man speaking to him about honoring his oath as guardian. How he would face the consequences if he did not honor that oath.

"Damon, as guardian, broke his sworn oath as guardian. The man in the vision said the ley lines were breaking, and the magic would rise. What if his oath as guardian was to absorb that magic?" she said.

"But your grandmother interfered. You told me she said the magic had to go somewhere," he said.

She nodded. "Yes, and she used the cloak to capture the magic, stealing it from him. Because the rising magic, if it was not contained somehow, would destroy the village. So, in a sense, she stole the magic, protected the village, and Damon's broken oath enacted the curse."

It was something she ruminated over since her grandmother told her the story. Now, it seemed to all make sense to her. Rowan stared at her from across the fire, the flickering light on his face as he contemplated her words. As she looked at him, it struck her how handsome he was. He'd never said why he wanted to help her but as they looked at each other, she wondered if his fate was tied to the dire wolf's. Was he, like Damon, cursed? Was his fate tied to the Wolf King's curse?

Then he said, "You intend to break the curse. Not kill him."

"I...I don't know. If the curse breaks and he's returned to a man, then what happens to him? Does he remember all that he did? Does he know who he is or was? Will he continue his bloodthirsty vendetta?"

"Only Damon knows the answer to that. You and I will never know until the curse breaks." He pulled out the provisions her grandmother had packed and broke off a piece of bread. He handed it to her.

She took it as her stomach rumbled.

"How do you intend to break the curse?" he asked.

As she stared into the fire holding the bread, she realized there was only one way to do it. Only one way to release the magic within it and—hopefully—break the curse.

"I have to destroy the cloak."

CHAPTER 7

In an ancient temple, in the far reaches within the Glenwood Forest, magic reigned supreme. Dark magic, light magic, controlled magic, uncontrolled magic, all magic. It seeped from the stone walls carved with archaic symbols—that which kept this amalgamation in check—swirling about in an otherworldly miasma. A pungent, sharp odor permeated the air. Overhead, a small opening allowed a slash of light to push back the shadows, illuminating the man sitting cross-legged on the stone dais. All around him, tiny sparkling particles danced within the light.

The temple, protected by runes and symbols, was the repository. A dumping ground for the consolidation of the various magics.

His arms extended outward from his body, his palms facing up. The sparkling magic gathered on his hands like dew drops in the dawn. As it seeped into his palms, a tingling sensation erupted through him. It clung to him, making his olive-toned skin shimmer.

This was only the beginning. The ley lines were coming to life once again. The ancient temple coming to life was the first sign. The first sign that it was time for him, as guardian, to absorb that magic and release it into the temple. To keep it safe and out of the hands of those who would do harm with it.

However, there was a price to pay. The destruction was imminent. He would, without thought or care, watch the ley lines break apart the small village, the earth expelling the magic in a fantastic fashion as though it were a volcano erupting molten lava.

If he did not take this wroth magic into his own self, as guardian, then the chaos in its wake would be cataclysmic.

The dream came to him this way every night. And every night, Damon awoke in the skin of the dire wolf. He was no longer a man. Every day, a little more of his humanity slipped away.

Seeing the girl with the red cloak, however, gave him renewed hope. Hope that he could finally be released from his feral curse and returned to the man. Hope that she would help him.

He searched for a way to regain his humanity for years. And now, this girl with the red cloak was his salvation. He knew who she was. He recognized the cloak, scented the sharp tang of its magic. Her face was familiar—high cheekbones, pert nose, wide eyes. Eyes that matched the woman he once loved.

The woman who betrayed him to save all that she loved. The woman who forced him to forsake his oath and bound him in this cursed four-legged body. The woman on whom he intended to exact his revenge.

He returned to this ancient temple, now crumbling from decay. But the runes carved into the walls were still intact. The magic the stones harbored was still there, dormant. Waiting for his return to human form. Waiting for the day he could release it.

That day was coming.

Poppy awoke with a start. She sat up, momentarily disoriented until she recalled where she was. The fire Rowan built was nothing more than embers now. Sunlight drifted through the cracks in the roof overhead, slashing down into the one-room cottage. Dust motes danced happily within the light.

Across from her, Rowan still slept, curled on the dirt floor. His face was in repose, his breathing deep. A lock of dark hair fell over his forehead. She admired him as he slept, wondering if they had met under different circumstances if there would be a chance for them to be together.

She shoved away those romantic thoughts. In all her years, falling in love had never been at the top of her list.

Rowan stirred. His eyes blinked open and met hers across the red coals. She instantly wished she had looked away but now found she could not. A strange feeling passed over her. A curious swooping went through her. Deep in his eyes, she saw his own feelings reflected back to her. Caring. Concern. Fear. It touched her in a way she had never been touched before. Her gut twisted. Her heart pounded.

"Good morning," he said, his voice soft and low.

"Good morning," she replied, finding her voice. She pushed to her feet, grabbing her longbow in the same motion. "Shouldn't we be going?"

"Food first," he said.

At that, her stomach rumbled. He reached for the food rations and pulled out bread, cheese, dried fruit. He offered her a portion of each. She took it, returning to the floor opposite him. They ate in silence until she could no longer stand the quiet.

"What is our plan today?" she asked. "I thought you only wanted to move under the cover of darkness."

"I'm rethinking that," he said.

He munched on a piece of fruit, his eyes distant. He was deep in thought, likely considering all their options and trying to select the best one. When he looked at her again, that curious swooping flashed through her again and she suppressed an inward groan.

Yes, he was handsome. She acknowledged that.

Yes, he was helping her. She acknowledged that, too.

No, nothing would ever be between them. It simply did not make sense.

"There is an ancient temple that is said to be the home of the Wolf King," he said.

She lifted a brow. "You've never mentioned this before."

"I wasn't certain we should go there," he said. "It is dangerous."

"No more dangerous than hunting the dire wolf," she pointed out.

"Yes, but the temple is no ordinary temple." He paused, took a bite of cheese. "There is magic there. Wild, ancient magic."

She peered at him across the disappearing fire, questions pounding through her.

"It is the temple of the guardian," he said.

"What does that mean?" she asked.

"It means that when the guardian takes in the magic from the breaking ley lines, he takes it there to release it. Think of it as a repository for all that wild unfettered magic. I think this is where the Wolf King would return."

"You mean, Damon in the form of the Wolf King," she said.

After a moment of consideration, he nodded. "Yes, I believe he would go there. He would know to go there because that's where he would have released the magic from the village's ley lines."

"Until my grandmother stopped him," she said.

And the direct result of his curse.

"I think we will find him there," Rowan said.

"And if he's not, we wait for him." It wasn't a question.

"As I said, it's a dangerous place."

She ate the rest of her rations and snatched her weapon. "Then what are we waiting for?"

Smiling, he rose and kicked dirt on the glowing embers to snuff it out. Then he packed up the rest of their rations, ready to depart.

She pulled the hood over her head and followed him out into the cool morning.

Chapter 8

Rowan led them deeper into the forest as the day waned. She'd never been so far from home as she was at that moment. The more distance she put between her and her village gave her a sense of unease. As though she'd never make it back home.

But did she really want to go back home? After what her grandmother told her about the Wolf King and her parents, the betrayal and the quest for justice was thrust upon her. Once she found this elusive dire wolf and broke the curse, what then? What would become of her?

Shoving those thoughts aside, she decided to think about that another day. Not now. The apprehension was already pounding hard through her. She didn't need to add to her anxiety with thoughts of what was to come after this was all over.

"You're quiet," Rowan said, casting her a look over his shoulder.

"How much farther?" she asked.

"Not far now."

There was a rustling in the surrounding woods. Rowan halted, his keen eyes peering into the afternoon shadows. She stopped right behind him, her heart suddenly in her throat. Through the magic of the cloak, she sensed something out there. Something watching and waiting for them. Something that was not friendly. She slid her longbow off her shoulder and gripped it, ready to use it if necessary.

"Rowan—" she started.

He held a hand up to silence her as he kept his watchful gaze on the surrounding foliage. The rustling sounded again to their left followed by a low rumble. Rowan's gaze met hers. She started to tell him they were in danger, that they should run.

She had enough time to reach for an arrow when all hell broke loose. The animal leapt from its hiding spot onto the path in front of them, baring its teeth and snarling.

It was a dark gray wolf.

Not the Wolf King.

Rowan pushed her behind him as if she needed protecting. As she reached for an arrow from her quiver, the wolf charged him.

Lighting quick, he turned to give her a mighty shove backward away from him. Then he shifted. Watching him transform from man to beast was mesmerizing. He tipped forward as his body morphed into a black wolf. He stood with his legs apart, his head lowered, and his teeth gnashing and snapping at the other one. The two beasts were in a standoff.

As Poppy decided what to do next, she sensed something moving through the brush. She turned to her right, peering through the forest. Gold eyes pierced her. She heard his muffled roar as their eyes met.

The Wolf King.

The cloak stirred against her skin, its fibers shimmering faintly like before, alive with the same magic that always felt out of her grasp.

She was in trouble.

She nocked an arrow as the dire wolf leapt toward her. She stumbled backward, emitting a choked cry. He was on her in an instant. Her instincts took over. She dropped her longbow and lifted her arms as the wolf attacked, teeth snapping and gnashing.

She stumbled away from him. Her hood fell back. The material of the red cloak fluttered behind her as the wolf pushed her back and back and back. She tripped over a thick branch, losing her footing and falling. The dire wolf seized the opening, launching forward in a blur of fur and teeth.

All she saw was teeth and fur. The feral odor of wolf permeated the air. The next thing she knew, the dire wolf yelped and turned his attention to something else. Something that attacked him from behind.

It was Rowan in his wolf form.

"Rowan, no!" she shouted.

But it was too late for that. The two beasts locked in battle in a blur of activity—a mass of gray and black fur as they fought each other. The other wolf joined the fray and then it was even more difficult to see what was happening.

Poppy searched for her longbow. She had dropped it when the Wolf King charged her. Now, she scrambled for it. She snatched it up, grabbed the arrow and nocked it. In one fluid movement, she let it fly, hoping she wouldn't hit Rowan.

A high-pitched yelp as the arrow found its mark. The other wolf. The arrow stuck out of its shoulder as it hobbled away, leaving Rowan and the Wolf King fighting each other.

She nocked another arrow, trying to get off a clean shot, but it was almost impossible. Rowan bit down on the Wolf King's shoulder. He yelped in pain and tried to attack him back. Then Poppy had a clear shot. She took it.

The arrow landed on its mark—in the back hip of the Wolf King. His head whipped around toward her showing his teeth, ready to pounce despite the arrow sticking out of him. He let out a deep, guttural sound, those gold eyes wild with fear, pain, and anger. She took a few steps backward, intending to run, but it was too late.

The enormous dire wolf leapt.

Her cloak continued to shimmer and glow.

He was on her in a flash. She threw up her hands to block him, but his teeth tore at her flesh. She cried out with the pain, trying to shove him off but it was almost impossible. He was big and strong and wild.

He let out another yelp as Rowan bit one of his hind legs.

It gave Poppy enough time to flip over and frantically crawl away. But the Wolf King landed on her again, shoving her against the ground and snapping at her head. She covered her head with her hands, trying to protect herself. Teeth tore into the flesh of her hands.

She wasn't sure what happened then. But she heard more yowling, more snarling, more growling. As though there were other wolves in the area. Then the Wolf King was gone. She rolled to her side, her hands bleeding from the wounds and saw a pack of wolves surrounding the dire wolf.

The dire wolf used his massive size to get away from them, injuring several of them. He bounded away, his back haunches bleeding from bite-marks and the arrow still sticking out of him. He crashed through the underbrush and disappeared once again into the wild. As soon as he was gone, her cloak stopped shimmering.

Several of the wolves who came to help limped away. Another remained on the ground, panting.

It was Rowan.

A strangled gasp escaped her.

She crawled toward him, ignoring her bleeding hands, her shredded tunic. He emitted a faint whimper as she reached him, placing a hand on his thick fur and feeling the slow beat of his heart. The Wolf King had torn a chunk of flesh out of him. He was bleeding.

"Rowan!" She said his name on a gasp. Her hand landed on his head, stroking him between his ears to comfort him. "Stay with me."

His eyes turned to her, blinked once, twice, then closed. As though he were giving up. Fumbling, she reached into her pocket for the healing tincture her grandmother gave her. With shaking hands, she uncorked it. She had no idea how to administer it to the wolf, but she had to try.

She scooted closer, pulling his head into her lap. With one hand, she managed to nudge open his mouth. Then she dribbled a bit of the tincture on his tongue, hoping it would help. She pushed his muzzle closed.

"Please don't die," she whispered. "You promised to keep me safe. Remember?"

When his eyes didn't open, she tried again. She poured more of the tincture into his mouth. Then, for good measure, she scattered a few drops on his wound.

"I can't do this without you," she said, patting him.

Looking up, she realized three wolves sat in a semi-circle. They must have come to help. They peered at her, watching, curiosity glinting in their wolf eyes. One threw back its head and howled. The other two followed.

Maybe these wolves were part of Rowan's pack.

How had he shifted? Did the tincture her grandmother give him wear off?

With a gentleness, she pushed his head onto the ground. Then she curled onto her side next to him, her hand in the thick mass of fur at his neck. The three wolves continued to sit and watch, as though guarding them. As the sun dipped toward the horizon, her eyes grew heavy. Before long, she was fast asleep.

CHAPTER 9

Birds twittered their early morning song. Deep in the ancient woods, an animal scurried through the underbrush, the leaves crackling with its movement. A breeze rustled the treetops, disturbing the solace of the branches.

Poppy heard all this as she awoke, her senses alerting her to nature around her.

The first thing she noticed was the cold ground underneath her. The second thing was the throbbing pain in her hands.

When she opened her eyes, she was looking at a familiar face. Rowan. He had shifted back into his human form.

He slept. He'd lost his cloak. Perhaps he'd shed it before he shifted into a wolf. The shoulder of his tunic was ripped. She saw with some horror the claw marks slashed across his shoulder. They were pink as if newly healed. He was no longer bleeding, which was a relief. The healing tincture she sprinkled into his mouth and on his shoulder helped.

She sat up, her body objecting to the movement. Her back ached from sleeping on the ground all night. Her head throbbed. When she lifted her shaking hand to rub her forehead, she saw it was crusted with blood where the Wolf King bit her.

She searched for the tincture. She must have dropped if after administering it to Rowan. She found it on the ground between them, the liquid drained. She'd forgotten to put the cork back in the bottle. Frowning, she dropped it back to the ground.

Movement caught her attention. Looking over Rowan's prone form, she saw three wolves. One sat up, stretching his long legs and yawning. The other two sensed its movement and rose, too. The three of them sat on their haunches and peered at her with dark eyes. They made no other movement toward her or Rowan.

"You stayed here all night," she said, her voice hoarse. "You kept watch over us, didn't you?"

The one in the middle, the largest, got to all fours and padded toward them. She stiffened as the animal approached. It sniffed Rowan's head then emitted a little whimper as if worried about him.

Rowan groaned and rolled to his back, opening his eyes. The wolf stood over him and then gave his cheek a little lick. Grinning, Rowan reached for the wolf and ruffled his fur around his neck.

"I'm all right," he said to the wolf.

The wolf licked him again. The other two wolves joined the first, sitting behind it as if waiting their turn.

Poppy remained still as she watched the exchange, marveling at the interaction. Rowan continued to pet the wolf as if it were nothing more than a domesticated dog.

He sensed her looking at him. When their eyes met, words froze in her throat. They stared at each other in silence for a long moment as he gave the wolf one last pat.

"Go on, now," he said to the wolf.

It dipped its head as if in acknowledgment and turned. The three wolves padded back to the woods and disappeared within the leaves.

Poppy wasn't sure what she witnessed, but she understood it was something special. Rowan looked back at her. Silence hung thick between them as they stared at each other. Finally, he looked away and inspected his clothes. The torn tunic exposed his shoulder.

She busied herself with collecting her longbow. He noticed her wounded hands and crawled toward her, reaching for her. His cold hands gripped hers.

"You're hurt," he said.

She tried to tug away. "I'm fine."

"He hurt you." His thumb grazed the back of her hand with a gentle touch. "Where's the healing tincture?"

Flushing hot, she looked at the discarded bottle between them. He released her and picked it up but immediately saw it was empty.

"I forgot to cork it after I used it on you," she said.

His features softened. "You didn't take any for yourself?"

"No," she said, swallowing hard. "I was more concerned about you."

His expression was unreadable as he clutched the empty bottle between his hands. "Poppy..."

She shoved to her feet, trying to ignore the way he looked at her. It made her insides quiver. "It's nothing to worry about."

"It's not nothing. Let me see your hands." He dropped the bottle and got to his feet. He held out his hand for hers.

"I—"

"Now, please."

It was the please that got her and the stern tone of his voice. She held her hands out to him. Taking them in his, he inspected the wounds.

"Wait here."

He searched the area. He found his cloak and snatched it off the ground, draping it over his arm. He found the waterskin and slung it over his shoulder. Then he ripped the lining out of his cloak, tearing it into long pieces. He doused one of the pieces in water and reached for her hand again.

Gently, he cleaned the dried blood away with the damp cloth.

"It's not deep," he said.

When the blood was cleaned off her hands, he used the other strips of cloth as a makeshift bandage, wrapping it round her hands and tying it off.

"There. That should keep the wounds clean until we can properly dress them."

She watched in silence as he pulled the ruined cloak on over his shoulders. Then he picked up the knapsack with their provisions, acting as if nothing else was amiss.

"We should be going." He headed for the trees.

"Rowan, are we going to talk about what happened last night?"

Halting, he turned back to her. Color tinged his cheeks. "What's to talk about?"

Stunned, she huffed. "Everything. The Wolf King, the other wolves. You." When he didn't answer, she added, "You shifted. I thought you said my grandmother gave you something to keep you from doing that."

He licked his lips and looked away, not wanting to answer.

"The Wolf King attacked you. I had to do something," he finally said.

Her brows drew together in question. "I don't understand."

"I told you I'd protect you," he said. "I made a promise. I intend to keep that promise."

"Rowan—"

"It was the only way." He took two steps toward her, pausing in front of her. "Yes, your grandmother gave me the tincture to keep me from shifting. But I didn't take it."

Shock rolled through her. "You lied?"

"I merely pretended to drink it. She doesn't understand how powerful he is. I can fight him best in wolf form. It was the only way to keep you safe." He reached for her bandaged hand and took it in his, holding her fingers loosely to not hurt her. "And you're right. You can't do this without me."

Her gut clenched. He'd heard her? When he was in wolf form? She reeled from that information as he granted her a knee-melting smile. He reached for her hand, taking it in his warm one. Her heart skipped at the small gesture.

"Thank you for saving my life," he said, softly.

His voice was low, steady, and laced with something she couldn't quite name—but it pulled at her, making her knees suddenly unsteady.

Oh, her stupid, traitorous heart skipped again, a wild flutter that made her chest feel too tight. Heat rushed up her neck like a firestorm, spreading to her cheeks and scorching all the way to the tips of her ears. She was sure her face was as red as the setting sun, and she prayed he couldn't see how flustered she was.

"You're welcome."

They stood there, locked in place, the space between them crackling with an unspoken tension. His hand was warm around hers, firm yet achingly gentle, and she was all too aware of the calluses on his fingertips brushing against her skin.

Poppy couldn't breathe, couldn't think. Her heart pounded so loudly it drowned out everything else. She swore the air shifted, thickening around them, pulling them closer even though neither of them moved. Was it her imagination? Or had something between them truly changed in that charged, fragile moment?

She didn't know whether to break the silence or let it linger. Every second felt like an eternity. Then, slowly, almost reluctantly, he let go of her hand.

The absence of his touch left her cold, and she didn't realize how tightly she'd been holding her breath until it came out in a shaky exhale.

"So," she said, her voice strained as she fumbled to regain her composure. "What do we do now?"

"We continue searching for the Wolf King."

"He was injured," she said, "when he left."

"Then he'll go directly to the temple to heal. We have a good chance of finding him there if we hurry."

He started the trek back into the forest. Taking a deep breath, she followed.

Chapter 10

They walked all day, only pausing a few times to stop for food and water. Then they were on their way again without a lot of chatter.

Poppy was busy thinking about everything that happened with Rowan. The way he looked at her after the Wolf King attack. The way he bandaged and then held her hand. It sent her senses reeling and she wasn't sure what to make of that.

All her life, she trained for one thing and one thing only—hunting down and killing the Wolf King. Despite his attack, she knew without a doubt she would not kill him. He was acting on instinct and he must sense the magic in her cloak. That was why he was drawn to her. Everything inside her wanted to break the curse, turning him back into a man and allowing him to be free.

Nor was she sure what to make of the other wolves who came to their aid when they were under attack. She wanted to ask more questions about that but lacked the courage. Rowan didn't seem to be terribly forthcoming with information either. So, she was content to remain silent, a prisoner of her swirling thoughts as she grappled with these sudden amorous feelings.

Falling in love was never top of mind for her. And now, here was Rowan, with his shaggy black hair, his soft smile, his adoring eyes. It made her insides quiver. But what future did they have together? He was a shifter, after all. When all this was over, he would return to wherever he came from. It occurred to her, then, she didn't *know* where he came from or why he was there that morning in the woods when she first spotted the Wolf King.

The sun dipped toward the horizon, casting long, cool shadows on the forest floor and through the trees. Night was upon them.

Rowan came to a halt near a fallen log, his keen eyes glancing around the area as he paused to peer into the foliage.

"I think we should stop here tonight," he said.

"What about the temple?" She still clutched her longbow in one hand, constantly on edge that another wolf attack would come. It never did.

"It's not far now," he said. He dropped the knapsack near the log. "We should reach it in the morning."

She watched as he started to gather firewood. She dropped her weapon next to the knapsack to help. Every time she got close to him, her cheeks warmed. Which was ridiculous! She was not the type of girl to swoon when coming into close proximity to a man.

But he wasn't just any man, was he? He was a shifter. And in his wolf form, he was fierce.

And he was her protector.

"Ah, thanks," he said with a grin when she handed him the gathered firewood.

Their hands brushed, making her heart flutter. Again, ridiculous. Her words were frozen in her throat, so she merely gave him a nod to say *you're welcome*. Then she sat on the ground with her back against the log and busied herself with rationing their food while he built a fire.

When he was done, and the fire was blazing brightly, he stood with his back to her staring into the woods. His hands were by his sides, fisted. He cocked his head to one side, listening. Then he looked at her over his shoulder.

"Stay here," he said.

Alarm hammered through her. "Where are you going?"

"I'll be right back," he called as he disappeared into the woods, the shadows swallowing up his form.

She froze, her heart ramming hard in her chest as she held her breath and waited for his return. She tuned into the magic of the cloak to listen to their surroundings.

There was the twitter of a nightingale somewhere in the distance. The crickets were singing. Nocturnal animals were foraging. A brook babbled over rocks. And then she heard something—a larger animal—moving through the underbrush in the direction Rowan disappeared.

She reached for her longbow, clutching it in her clammy palm as she continued to listen.

He whispered something in the wind. Words she could not hear. Her brows drew together. What was he doing?

Then footsteps and he reappeared at the edge of the trees on the other side of the fire. The light flickered over his handsome, chiseled face as his dark, glittering eyes landed on her. They stared at each other for several hard heartbeats.

"Everything all right?" she asked. Her voice was steadier than she anticipated.

His shoulders relaxed. "All is well."

She relaxed her grip and released the weapon as he sat next to her. She handed him his rations for the night. They ate in silence.

But as she sat there, peering into the place he'd gone, she saw two glowing eyes peering back at her. Her gut clenched. Another pair of eyes to the left of that one. And then another.

Three.

Three wolves.

She stiffened, her hand landing on her longbow, ready to wield it.

"There's nothing to fear," he said, sensing her unease. "They're here to protect us."

He placed a hand on her arm in reassurance. She'd crushed the piece of bread in her fist and hadn't realized it.

"Who are they?" she asked.

He popped a piece of cheese in his mouth, chewing thoughtfully before answering. "My pack."

Understanding thumped through her. These three wolves were the ones who came to their aid when they fought the Wolf King. She removed her hand and placed it in her lap.

"You spoke to them, didn't you?" she asked, watching the glittering eyes peering back.

"They will not harm you," he said.

He'd kept his eyes cast downward as he ate. Now he lifted his head to look at her. That one look held so much meaning. He truly did intend to protect her, and he was using his pack to help guard them throughout the night.

"They've been following us all day," he said. "You didn't know?"

She shook her head. She should have been in tune with the surrounding nature through the magic of the cloak, but she was too preoccupied with her own thoughts and feelings to pay attention to anything other than that.

"Are they like you?" she asked.

He fiddled with the food he held. "Somewhat."

"What does that mean?"

"They're cursed."

She stifled a gasp. "Like the Wolf King?" Which made her wonder, "Are you?"

Rowan granted her a weak smile. "Like the Wolf King."

He didn't answer her question about himself. If the Wolf King's curse was broken, and he was cursed as well, then what? Would he be man or beast? What would happen to his pack?

"If they're cursed, too, then..." Her words trailed off as she peered at the three pair of eyes looking back at them from the forest.

"There is more you should know, yes," Rowan said, as if answering a question she didn't ask.

She waited for him to continue. He finished his bread and brushed crumbs from his pants. Then he settled back against the log, folding his arms over his chest.

"You know the story of the village with the ley lines," he said. "How the magic erupted and there was nowhere for it to go."

She nodded.

"Something happened that day. Not all the magic was absorbed into that cloak you wear. A bit of it seeped from the ley lines into the air. That bit of magic was part of Damon's curse." He gave her a sideways look. "And part of that curse affected others."

"Others? You mean, you?"

"Me. Them." He pointed with his chin to the three wolves standing guard keeping a watchful eye on their small camp. "They cannot shift like I can. But they were once men."

Her mouth had suddenly gone dry as the pieces of the puzzle started to fall into place. "You were in the woods that morning looking for me, weren't you?"

"I was tracking the Wolf King," he said. "I thought if I found him, I'd find you. Turns out you found me first." He gave her a sheepish grin.

Poppy stared into the fire, trying to make sense of it all. "You *want* me to break the curse."

"I want you to do what you think is right," he said. "But I ask you to break the curse. To free those of us who cannot free ourselves."

She thought back to that morning in the woods when she shot him with her arrow. How he had initially resisted coming with her back to the cabin, but then agreed. He knew who she was all along just as he knew who her grandmother was. How long had he looked for her? Days? Months? Years? And how convenient it was for her to shoot him with her arrow that morning.

Coincidence or kismet?

"Your offer to help me then was self-serving," she said, trying not to sound accusatory.

"Not selfish, no." He dropped his arms and turned to her, angling his body to look at her. "I *wanted* to help you find him. I thought if I helped you hunt him down, that if he died..." He pressed his lips together.

"That it would break the curse," she said, finishing for him.

He nodded, guilt slashing over his face. "But I no longer believe killing him will break the curse. Not if your cloak is tied to him and his magic."

"Why didn't you tell me the truth?" she asked.

"I didn't know if I could trust you," he said.

She peered at him, trying to decide how to feel about this new information. "And now?"

Contemplation flickered over his face as he searched her face trying to decide how to answer. He swallowed hard. "I trust you with my life. I'll protect you until my dying breath with mine."

As he said it, their eyes met. His vow shimmered between them more than an oath. It was a declaration. The magic of the cloak attuned to her senses, and she saw something more than a promise to keep her safe buried deep in those dark eyes of his. It made her question everything about her life to this point. She'd forsaken love for vengeance.

It was not vengeance she sought anymore. It was absolution for her grandmother's past wrong doings. A burden she never wanted nor expected to have.

Breaking the curse was no longer narrowed to the Wolf King. Rowan and his pack depended on her success or failure. The weight of that pressed on her, pulsing through her in a way for which she was never prepared.

Finally, she said, "What is the plan when we reach the temple in the morning?"

"The magic in the temple is ancient. It will likely work against us. You said yourself you had to destroy the cloak to break the curse. We'll find a way to do that."

"I'm not sure it will work," she said. Destroying the cloak was hypothetical. There was no way to truly know if it would work.

"We'll find a way," he said, sounding strong and sure. "If the Wolf King is there, he'll use everything at his disposal to keep you out of the temple. He'll want to get that cloak off you to use against us. Try not to let him have it."

She chewed on her lower lip. "You certainly know a lot about this."

"I've had years to track down the answers. To find a way to break the curse."

Meaning, it's taken him years to find her. It seemed Nana hid them well from the outside world for a lot of years while filling her head with tales of the terrible Wolf King.

"We should get some sleep," he said then. "We'll want to be rested for tomorrow."

She nodded. Sleeping on the ground wasn't exactly her favorite thing, but she knew there was no other choice. It gave her some comfort to know Rowan's pack was out there watching over them.

She settled against the ground, her arms under her head as she faced the fire. Rowan rolled over, his back to her. And before too long, she was fast asleep.

CHAPTER 11

Poppy awoke during the night, listening to the quiet. There was a stillness about the air that was disconcerting. No crickets chirped. No nocturnal creatures foraged.

She sat up. The fire had turned to nothing more than glowing embers. She peered into the darkness. The three sets of glowing eyes peered back.

That, at least, gave her some comfort. The wolves were still there, guarding them.

She rested against the fallen log, thinking about the coming morning. How would she handle things once they reached the temple? Would the Wolf King be there? If he wasn't, then what? And what about Rowan?

She had a lot of pressure on her now, knowing that breaking the curse would also release Rowan and his pack mates from their forced captivity. She never wanted that responsibility. But, then, she never wanted the responsibility of taking out the Wolf King in the first place, either.

In the east, the sun began its ascent. But the forest surrounding them was so thick, the sunbeams didn't penetrate the woods. She only knew it was dawn by the sound of the morning birds twitter-ing. She clutched her elbows, pulling her cloak tight around her, to ward off the morning chill since the fire had long since burned out.

She no longer saw the glowing eyes on the edge of the trees. Perhaps the three wolves had decided their duty was done.

Next to her, Rowan stirred. He rolled to his side and then sat up. His hair was mussed. His eyes were sleepy. His clothes were rum-pled. The ripped tunic hung off his shoulder revealing his golden skin and the healing pink scar where the dire wolf attacked him. Beneath that ripped tunic she saw the strength of his upper body. Heat pounded through her as she quickly looked away, searching for her discarded longbow.

"You're awake," he said.

"I've been awake for some time." She snatched up the longbow and reached for the quiver of arrows, slinging it over one shoulder as she hoisted to her feet. "We should be going. It's dawn."

"Do you want to break your fast?" he asked, reaching for the knapsack.

Her stomach was in knots. She wasn't sure she could eat. She shook her head.

Rowan said nothing as he grabbed the knapsack of food and got to his feet. He arranged his cloak around his frame, ran a hand through his tousled hair, and then inspected the fire to make sure it was out. There must have been a few glowing embers for he kicked dirt over it to snuff it. Smoke curled in lazy tendrils from the charred wood.

"Ready?" he asked.

She gave him a nod. "As I'll ever be."

Nodding, he led them away from their makeshift camp into the forest. She followed him through the thick trees and overhanging branches as the songbirds continued their morning rituals and the forest came alive. A slash of morning light filtered through the treetops in places, illuminating the tiny creatures floating through the light looking for their breakfast.

Poppy's stomach, meanwhile, rumbled. She regretted her refusal of food but then, she was ready to face the Wolf King and put it all behind her. The sooner she did, the sooner she could return home.

And then what? What would she do then? At that point, she'd fulfilled her life's destiny and completed the path her grandmother set her upon from the day her parents were killed.

These thoughts consumed her as they continued their trek. Rowan stopped so suddenly in front of her, she nearly ran into him. She halted, her body rigid and pulling to a quick stop to keep from plowing into his back. He stiffened, his head cocked to one side as he listened.

She listened, too, tuning into the sounds of the forest. They'd changed. No longer did she hear the happy songs of the birds or the fluttering of wings along the treetops. Here, there was nothing but a stillness that settled around them. A deep quiet, shrouding them in silence.

A rich, loamy scent filled the air with a hint of damp moss. But underneath that was something darker, more dangerous. Like the bitter metallic tang of blood or rusted iron. That wasn't all, though. Mingling with those scents were smokey, earthy smells. Like a damp cave, decaying leaves, or ancient stones. Like dusty parchment or old leather.

All of these hit her full force, pounding her olfactory sensors. She clenched her jaw, putting a hand to her head and squeezing her eyes shut as if that would help stop the onslaught of odor.

"What is that?" she whispered.

"We're here," he replied.

"Here?"

He nodded, his eyes sharp and assessing with a hint of dread. Then he took two steps forward and pushed aside a low-hanging branch to reveal aged stone covered in moss and lichen.

Poppy narrowed her eyes, trying to make sense of what she was seeing. It appeared to be nothing more than a stone wall. But then when he pushed aside more branches, clearing away the bracken, the temple revealed itself.

Strange symbols she had never seen before were carved into the ancient stone. Nearly worn smooth by time and age. Each stone on the wall had a different symbol from the ground to the top, which was so tall it disappeared into the shadowy treetops of the forest.

"Come," he said. "Follow me."

He placed a hand on the stone and followed the wall. She fell in step behind him, pulling an arrow from her quiver and nocking it, keeping it at the ready. Her heart thrummed a wild beat in her chest. Her breath was shallow and erratic.

Calm. She must be calm.

But she was steps away from approaching the Wolf King in his lair.

The wall gave way to an opening. It was nothing more than a crude doorway carved from the stone. Here, Rowan paused and stared into the gloominess of the temple. With her heart in her throat, she halted behind him and peered over his shoulder.

What appeared to be a low stone altar was in the center. Curled up on that altar was the gray dire wolf. He was too large for the stone. One back leg and his tail hung off. His eyes were closed as he slept. Dried blood caked his back haunches where she'd shot him with her arrow and where the other wolves bit him. The arrow was gone now. She hadn't any idea how the dire wolf managed to remove it without help.

Overhead, a slash of light illuminated the beast. Tiny, sparkling particles danced in the light, shimmering against the darkness and shadows.

There was that sharp, pungent odor again. It was coming from the temple itself.

A shiver of trepidation danced up her spine.

This was the moment she trained for all her life.

She never expected it would be in the dire wolf's lair.

Nudging Rowan to the side, she pulled her bow string taut and stepped around him, pointing the arrow directly at the wolf's head. A breath shuddered out of her as she held it. Her arm, though, was unsteady because she was shaking.

"Poppy?"

Rowan's voice behind her was quiet, tentative. As though he didn't understand what she was doing. She didn't understand it, either. But here she was, facing the moment she hurtled toward since she was a babe. The Wolf King murdered her parents and destroyed her life, taking away the two people who loved her the most. The two people who brought her into this world because they loved each other. The Wolf King turned Nana into a bitter, vengeful woman who wanted nothing more than to destroy him. He, in turn, nearly destroyed her.

So, Poppy pointed the arrow at the beast's head. All she had to do was release it. In one swift act, she'd rid the world of the vicious dire wolf while getting justice for her dead parents and her Nana.

"What are you doing, Poppy?" he asked, his voice a little stronger this time.

She didn't know what she was doing. Only that she was doing it.

The acrid smell of magic permeated her nose in that cloying scent that stuck to the back of her throat. Her breathing was erratic as she stared at the sleeping form of the dire wolf.

And then, her cloak began to shimmer like that day when the wolf shoved her to the ground and snarled in her face. The magic in the cloak sensed the magic in the temple.

The dire wolf lifted his head. His gold eyes met hers.

You've come at last.

The voice flickered through her mind. The same voice that spoke to her before. The one she heard that morning in the woods when she first spotted those glowing eyes.

They stared at each other for several heartbeats, her breath shuddering out of her. And then, slowly, she lowered the bow.

"I'm not going to kill you," she said.

Rowan stood still as a statue. His eyes were wide and round. His face had paled.

Foolish girl. His voice, dark and dangerous, flickered through her mind again.

"I am no fool," she said. "I want to help you."

"Are you—"

Silence the he-wolf. This is not his fight.

"But it *is* his fight," Poppy said. Rowan stood rigid with his hands fisted at his side. "He wants me to silence you."

"You can...You hear him?"

Her cloak continued to shimmer. She suspected it was the magic within the threads of the garment that allowed her to hear Damon speaking in her mind. But she didn't tell Rowan this. She turned her attention back to the dire wolf.

"I'm going to help you," she said again.

He laughed, a deep guttural laugh that resonated inside her mind. *You cannot help me, girl. That time has long passed.*

She dropped her weapon on the ground and held up her hands in surrender to show she was unarmed.

"You were a guardian once. You were in love with a woman named Ruby. But you couldn't be together because of who and what you are. Because of what you had to do."

The dire wolf rose to all fours and dropped his head to look at her, his eyes glowing. A feral snarl escaped him, his teeth flashing menacingly as a deep rumble vibrated from his massive chest.

You know nothing, girl.

"I know your name is Damon."

He continued to stare at her, though he didn't alter his stance. He remained standing on the rock, ready to pounce. She sensed the magic thrumming through the fibers of the cloak and knew it protected her. From him.

"The woman you loved...was my grandmother."

Enemy.

The dire wolf launched himself from the stone pedestal toward Poppy. She stumbled backward, wishing she hadn't released her weapon. Then, a flash of black fur was in front of her as Rowan in his wolf form leapt between her and the dire wolf baring his teeth.

"No, Rowan!"

But it was too late. They circled each other like two feral dogs. Both snarling and drooling. Their teeth bared.

Outside the temple, a howl sounded followed by another and another. The other three wolves had followed them here. Rowan's pack.

Inside the temple, the magic swirled within the slash of sunlight. Like a small cyclone, spinning and spinning and spinning. The sharp tang of it pierced her nose as she watched it whip into a frenzy. All the while Rowan and Damon faced off within the confines of the temple.

She snatched up her longbow, quickly nocking an arrow and pointing it at the dire wolf, waiting to get off a clean shot.

But the moment she was ready to fire, Damon leapt at Rowan.

They were nothing more than a blur of gray and black fur as they fought each other. Then a yip as the bigger, stronger dire wolf bit down on Rowan. She sucked in a breath as she pointed the arrow directly at Damon.

A commotion behind her caught her attention. She looked over her shoulder and saw the other wolves entering the temple, their teeth bared. They'd come to help Rowan. Now it was impossible to get a clear shot. Not with the other wolves in the mix.

She searched for something—anything—to help her. But the temple was devoid of anything else. All she had was her longbow, and it was useless to her now.

Meanwhile, the magic in the temple continued to whip into a frenzy. The smell of it was growing stronger—a mixture of earth, charred wood, sulfur, and the metallic tang of blood. The cloak around her shoulders warmed, turning hot. Hot enough for her to suck in a sharp breath and shove it off, letting it pool at her feet. She stepped away from it, watching as it pulsed bright red—like the hot coals of a dying fire.

The swirling magic within the temple dove for it, the shimmering particles hovering over the cloak, dancing around it as though it were ready to merge with the cloth.

The walls wept the same shimmering magic. It seeped from between the stones, seeking to join with the swirl hovering over her cloak. The cloak, it seemed, called to this magic within the temple.

A yowl caught her attention. Rowan was cowering away from the dire wolf. His black fur was damp—from blood. He whimpered as the other three wolves attacked Damon.

Poppy realized she had to do something, and quick. But what?

She saw the discarded knapsack of food on the ground. Next to it, his cloak where he'd torn out the lining to use as bandages for her hands. He limped toward the wall. His dark eyes met hers and she saw the pain and anguish deep within them.

Another glimpse of the crimson cape to see it pulsed bright as the swirling magic settled on the material, like morning dew drops.

An idea struck. She hurried to his cloak, dropped to her knees and searched the pockets. She found the matches and snatched them, turning back to the cloak shimmering on the ground, gathering the wild magic that fluttered down from the walls, the ceiling.

She gave Rowan one last look as he cowered against the wall. Then at Damon who was busy fighting with the three wolves. He wrapped his massive jaw around the neck of one and threw him to the side as though he weighed nothing. The wolf hit the wall with a yelp and then was silent. The other two whimpered and dashed away, leaving the temple.

Damon's golden eyes pierced her.

You will die now, girl.

Blood matted his gray fur—whether it was Damon's or the other wolves' didn't matter. She had one shot at this. She struck the match against the tinder box. A moment later, it flared to life in a bright yellow-white flame. She tossed the match onto the woven fibers of the enchanted cloak.

CHAPTER 12

The massive dire wolf threw his head back and released an ear-piercing howl.

As soon as the match hit the swirling magic hovering over the cloak, it ignited. A *whoosh* and then the entire cloak was engulfed in flames. The force of the flames was so hot, she stumbled back against the wall. The stifling heat filled the enclosed ancient temple. The dire wolf continued to howl.

Poppy inched her way down the wall to Rowan, still cowering on the ground near the back of the temple. As soon as her hand landed on him, she felt the damp blood.

He was big. Too big for her to carry him out of the temple.

"Rowan, you have to get up. We have to get out of here!"

His response was nothing more than a whine.

Behind her, the dire wolf continued to howl as he backed away from the flaming cloak. The swirling magic in the temple was driven to a fever pitch as it flooded out of the walls and ceiling.

Poppy put her arms around Rowan's neck. "I can't carry you. You have to get up."

His eyes fluttered open, half-lidded and glazed with pain, each slow blink tugging at her chest like a vice. He was broken—his breaths shallow, his face pale—and every second they lingered here was a death sentence.

The heat was unbearable, the air thick and suffocating as smoke curled through the crumbling temple. Sweat slicked her skin, but she didn't care. Panic clawed at her throat, threatening to choke her, but she forced it down. She couldn't fall apart. Not now.

"Stay with me," she whispered, her voice trembling as she crouched beside him. Her arms slid around his battered frame, her hands pressing into his thick fur as she tried to lift him.

He was so heavy, dead weight in her grasp, and her muscles screamed in protest. She gritted her teeth and pulled harder, her breaths coming out in sharp gasps.

"Come on," she pleaded through clenched teeth. "Don't do this to me. You're not dying here."

But it was no use. He didn't move, and her strength faltered. She wasn't strong enough. Tears burned in her eyes, more from frustration than the stinging smoke.

"No," she hissed, her voice breaking. Desperation surged through her, hot and wild, drowning out the rational part of her mind. She couldn't fail him. She wouldn't.

"Rowan, *please.*" Her face was damp from tears she didn't realize she'd shed.

A crack sounded behind her. She turned to see the fire growing and nearly reaching the ceiling. The dire wolf shook his head back and forth, back and forth, in pain. Red, white, yellow sparkles danced within the flames of the enchanted fibers as they slowly disintegrated within the blaze.

The dire wolf pitched to the side, flopping and convulsing. The shimmering magic emitted by the fire drifted down on him, like snow floating from the sky in lazy snowflakes. It gathered on him, covering his gray fur in a shimmering blanket. And then a flash of light ignited, lighting up the confines of the temple. It was so bright she had to shield her eyes.

Then the fire snuffed out, as if some unseen force had extinguished it. There was nothing left but a few remnants of charred cloth. And on the ground, the dire wolf was now a man.

A man curled on his side wearing tattered breeches and nothing more. His feet, chest, and arms were bare. He had a gash in his shoulder smeared with blood. His hair was long, gray, matted and covering his face.

Rowan, though, remained in wolf form. He hadn't shifted. The curse hadn't broken for him.

"Rowan!" She shook him, trying to rouse him.

His eyes fluttered open for only a moment, then closed again. His pants were shallow.

He was dying.

"No, Rowan!"

She buried her face in his fur and inhaled his damp, animal scent. And she realized then, that's what he smelled like the first time she met him. When he was no longer a wolf, but a man, with her arrow sticking out of his shoulder.

"Don't leave me, Rowan," she whispered against him. "You can't leave me alone in this world. I don't want to live without you."

He took one last breath, then...nothing.

She cried out as the pain lanced through her. "No!"

Then she buried her face in the thick fur of his neck once again, the wracking sobs overtaking her. She clutched his dampened pelt in her bandaged hands.

"He's dead, girl."

The dark, dangerous voice made her lift her head. She turned to see the man standing in the middle of the temple, his hands fisted by his side. His broad chest gleaming with sweat and blood. And his eyes—those gold, dangerous eyes—were fixed on her, glinting in the half-light of the shadowy temple.

This man was once the Wolf King.

Damon.

He sounded almost triumphant when he told her Rowan was dead. It sent a stabbing pain right to her heart and fury boiling through her veins.

"You." It was the only word she managed to spit out. Her voice was raw, raspy.

"Thank you for releasing me from the curse." He gave her a feral smile, showing all his teeth. "Now, I can finally exact my revenge on the woman who betrayed me all those long years ago."

She shot to her feet. "You will *not!*"

"She was once a formidable foe, but I suspect now she is old and frail. Isn't she?"

Poppy clenched her hands into tight fists, despite the pain of her injuries. The injuries he inflicted upon her when he was still a dire wolf. "You will stay away from her."

"Your grandmother, is it?" he continued, as if she hadn't spoken. "Of course, she is. You look much like Ruby. Strong and fierce and just as beautiful as she was once."

He stepped around the charred remains of her cloak and moved back to the stone dais. He lowered himself down to it, crossed his legs in front of him, and then placed his hands on his knees, closing his eyes.

"I tried to rid her of this world once. She bested me. She will never best me again."

He lifted his arms out to his side, palms up facing the roof of the small temple. She hadn't noticed until then the shimmering magic that swirled around her charred cloak. Now, it gathered along his bare arms, chest, shoulders, and palms as he called to it. He closed his eyes, sucked in a breath through his nose, and allowed the shimmering magic to seep into his skin.

The injuries from the wolf attack on his upper torso healed, closing the wounds.

He was gathering his strength. He was going to kill her. And then he was going to kill Nana.

Her discarded longbow lay between them, and doubt gnawed at her—could she reach it and wield it before he stopped her? Her heart beat wildly as fear punched her gut.

She had to take the chance.

Mustering her courage, she dove for the longbow. As soon as her hand landed on it, she snatched it up. Her discarded arrow was on the ground next to it. She grabbed it, but her hands shook too hard to nock the arrow.

"Still the foolish little girl, I see."

He charged her, shoving her against the wall of the temple. Her back thudded against the stone, knocking the wind out of her. His long, slender fingers wrapped around her wrist and pounded her hand against the stone. She cried out as the pain flared through her fingers, her wrist, her arm. She had no choice but to release her weapon.

But she still held the arrow in her other hand. She used her body weight to shove against him, giving herself enough space to slam the arrow into his shoulder.

He cried out and jerked back, stumbling away from her. She tried to turn and run but he was faster than she was. Stronger. He ripped the quiver from her back, the strap snapping as though it were made of nothing more than delicate paper. He tossed it aside, then snatched her long braid in one hand, jerking her back into him. Pain exploded through her scalp as she landed against his thick, solid chest. He wrapped an arm around her upper body. His other hand was on her throat, squeezing, trapping the air within her lungs. She gasped, trying to breathe, but he was crushing the life out of her and there was nothing she could do about it.

The edges of her visions narrowed, turning dark. Then starbursts exploded behind her eyes.

Suddenly, he shouted, released her. Poppy fell forward to her hands and knees, her eyes watering as she sucked in breath after breath. Her lungs burned.

Someone saved her. But who?

She turned her head and saw Rowan in human form on his feet, swaying, a blood-stained dagger in his hand, pointing it at Damon.

He wasn't dead!

As she tried to regain her strength, she watched in horror as they fought each other, hand to hand this time. Damon charged. Rowan swiped the dagger through the air, connecting with his forearm.

"You should be dead!" Damon spat.

Rowan said nothing as he charged again. Damon swatted his hand away, knocking the dagger from his grasp.

Poppy gathered her wits, saw her discarded longbow. She snatched it and frantically searched for her quiver of arrows. It was across the temple. She dove for it, her hands fumbling as she jerked an arrow free, nocked it, and spun in one fluid motion.

Damon had Rowan in a headlock, suffocating him.

She steadied her breath, aimed, and fired. The arrow landed with a thump against the base of Damon's skull.

He immediately fell forward, taking Rowan down with him and collapsing on top of him. Poppy dropped her weapon and hurried to him, shoving the dead man off him.

"Rowan!"

His dark eyes were bloodshot and watery. He reached for her, pulling her into his embrace, and holding her tight. So tight. His breath see-sawed in and out of him, his heart pounding hard and fast against her. She clung to him, thankful he was alive.

Finally, he released her, pulled back to look at her. They stared at each other for a long, quiet moment. Without the magic of the cloak to assist her, she was no longer able to read the depth of his eyes. She didn't need it. She saw relief and tenderness in his gaze.

"Are you hurt?" he asked.

She shook her head. "Rowan, I—"

It was as far as she got when he pulled her to him and kissed her. The suddenness of it took her breath away, but she welcomed it. She melted into him, savoring the warmth of his lips, the intoxicating sweetness of his taste. It was a kiss she had unknowingly yearned for her entire life, and now that it was here, it felt like coming home.

When they broke, he refused to release her. Her heart fluttered and her stomach twisted into tight knots.

"I thought you were dead," she managed to say.

"I thought I was, too, but something strange happened to me. Can you smell the sharp tang of magic?"

She sniffed the air and nodded. "Yes."

He brushed the back of his hand over her cheek. "It spoke to me."

Her brows drew together in question. "What did?"

"The magic. The voice was..." He paused, trying to decide how to describe it. "Like starlight and shadows all mixed into one. It said that though the curse was broken, Damon was not the man he once was. It told me." He paused again, swallowed hard. "I had to live to save the woman who broke the curse. I think the magic healed me, Poppy. I think it saved me."

Her cheeks flooded with heat as she remembered what she said when she thought he was gone. At the time, she was overcome with emotion and didn't guard her thoughts.

"Did you mean it?" he asked, his voice soft. "Did you mean you didn't want to live without me?"

Her heart thudded against her chest as a relentless beat echoing against her inner turmoil. A euphoric tingling sensation coiled in the pit of her stomach. She stood on the precipice of her own truth, no longer a prisoner to her fears. In the span of a few fleeting days, he had ignited something within her, a spark that grew into a fierce, undeniable desire. She wanted to stay with him, to weave their lives together for all the days to come.

"Yes," she said. "I meant it."

He smiled then. A smile that ignited the life in his eyes. He leaned in to kiss her again when a voice stopped him.

"Are you two finished swooning over each other?"

A man stood in the doorway to the temple. A man she didn't know. He wore tattered clothes. His feet were bare. His brown hair was long and shaggy. His face was thin and gaunt with dark circles under his dark eyes. She understood who he was—he was one of the wolves in Rowan's pack.

Rowan moved to get to his feet, helping her up, too.

"Poppy, this is Louis."

Louis reached for her bandaged hand, then, holding it gently between his. "Thank you, my lady."

She flushed and tugged her hand free. "No, I should be thanking you and the others."

His gaze flickered to the form on the floor by the wall of the temple. "I'm afraid Arthur didn't make it."

"Where's Frederick?" Rowan asked.

"He wanted to return home," Louis sifted from one foot to the other, clearly uncomfortable.

She didn't understand, but perhaps Rowan would explain it to her in time.

"We should destroy the temple," Louis said.

"But the guardians—" he began.

"There are other temples and other guardians," Louis said.

"How do we destroy it?" Poppy asked.

Louis was transfixed by the shimmering magic as it floated slowly to the ground, settling on Damon's lifeless form like snow blanketing a hilltop.

"The same way you destroyed the cloak," Louis said.

"We cannot destroy it," Rowan said. "It will release the magic within the walls into the world. It will be far more dangerous than leaving it."

Louis stared hard at him for a long, quiet moment as contemplation swept over his face. Finally, he nodded. "As you say."

Then he moved past them into the temple where the last wolf remained. He paused there, peering down at the lifeless body, his face creased with sadness. He hoisted the dead wolf in his arms and then headed for the door.

"I will bury Arthur."

It was the last thing he said as he disappeared out of the temple and into the forest.

Chapter 13

"I'm sorry about Arthur," Poppy said after a long moment.

"He died protecting you. He did what he needed to do. He wouldn't have wanted it any other way," he said. He reached down and picked up her longbow, handing it to her. "We should go."

"What about Damon?"

The shape on the ground was now covered in a sparkling mound of magic.

"We leave him and close up the entrance with rocks. The runes carved into the stone will keep the magic from releasing into the world."

He sounded so sure about that, she didn't question it. He clearly knew a lot more about Damon, the curse, and the magic than he ever told her.

Her quiver of arrows had been discarded, too, in the fight with Damon. She slung the longbow over her shoulder and picked up the quiver, ready to put this place behind her. Rowan retrieved his tattered cloak and pulled it on around his shoulders, then found the discarded knapsack with their meager rations.

"And once we do that?" she asked.

"Then," he gave her a small smile, "I take you home."

It took several hours to find enough rock to close up the entrance to the temple. For good measure, Rowan picked large branches to stack against the rocks to keep anyone from ever going back inside.

It was late in the day when they finally finished and started their trek back through the forest. The shadows were somehow not as dark or eerie now that she knew the Wolf King was gone.

She did wonder, though, what would happen when they returned to the village. Was he still able to shift into wolf form or was that gone now that the curse of the Wolf King was broken? Would Rowan bid her farewell and leave to try to regain his old life once again?

There were many questions swirling in her mind as they walked back through the forest long into the night. Fatigue pulsed through her. At one point, he looked back to see she was nearly dead on her feet and came to a halt.

"We should make camp," he announced.

He slid the knapsack off his shoulder and started to gather firewood. She helped and before too long, they had a fire blazing within the small circle of their cozy camp. Rowan divvied up the rations, handing her a slice of bread, cheese, and dried fruit. He held back a slice of each for himself. They ate in silence, as she peered into the fire, her eyes heavy with exhaustion. She fought back a yawn.

"Sleep, Poppy," he said.

She ate the rest of her rations. He poked the fire to keep it going.

"When the curse broke for the Wolf King...did it break for you, too?" she asked.

The reddish-orange light flickered over his face. "I can't say for sure, but I think so."

"Do you...feel different?" she asked, curious.

"Yes." He continued to poke the fire, encouraging the flames to go brighter and higher. "I no longer have that feral feeling pulsing just under the surface. As if any moment I'll change into the beast."

"You were no beast," she said around a yawn as she settled on the ground. She used her arms as a pillow. Her eyes drifted closed. "In fact, you were a lovely black wolf with the softest fur between your shoulder blades."

His chuckle was the last thing she heard before she drifted into sleep.

The following morning, after dousing the fire and sharing their rations, they headed back down the path of the forest. Poppy still had quite a few questions, but she remained quiet. Now that she was without her cloak, she realized there was a chill in the wind as they headed through the forest. When they paused for a quick break, Rowan noticed.

He removed his own tattered cloak and handed it to her. "Here. You need this more than me."

"I couldn't—"

"I insist."

When she refused to take it, he placed it around her shoulders. It was still warm from his body heat. She pulled it tight around her, happy for the warmth.

"Thanks."

"How are your hands?" he asked.

Glancing down, the crude bandages he'd tied around her hands were soiled from their fight with Damon.

"Let me see."

He reached for her, taking her hands in his. With a gentleness, he untied one and unwound it from around her palm. The wounds were healing and looked good but there was some bruising where the Wolf King bit her. He unwrapped the second one to see the same thing.

"Looks like you'll heal just fine." Still holding her hands, he granted her a smile.

Her heart fluttered. She liked the way her hand felt in his.

"Thanks to you," she said.

"Shall we continue?"

He motioned toward the path. She nodded and fell in step behind him. They walked in silence for a time until finally she could take it no more.

"Rowan, what did you do before you were...before the curse?"

"Before I was a wolf, you mean?" He grinned at her over his shoulder. "I was a blacksmith for King Rufus."

"You were?" she asked, surprised. "Then how did you—"

"How did I become cursed?"

She nodded.

"It was a strange thing that happened. The ley lines that ran through your grandmother's village also ran all the way to the castle right underneath my forge. I can only assume that when the eruption happened and Damon was unable to harness the wild magic, that something happened to me then. It was as though the magic burst forth from the ground, illuminating the forge all around me. I recognized the same magic back in the temple. The same shimmering, glittering magic. It smelled the same, too."

"That's how you know so much about this curse, then," she said.

"Yes, and why I left the forge after the first time I shifted. I knew I couldn't go back. And so, I made it my mission to find out what happened and why. I also discovered I was not the only one affected by this rogue magic."

"That's how you met Arthur, Louis and Frederick," she said.

"Yes, but I was only able to communicate with them when I was in wolf form. They were unable to shift back into human form at all."

It fascinated her to hear about this world outside of her own little one. The one in which she had been driven to hunt down and kill the Wolf King. Nana kept her sheltered and focused on her vengeance. Perhaps that was why she never ventured outside the village or why she never considered falling in love.

But now all that had changed. The Wolf King was dead. Rowan and his friends were human once again.

"What's wrong?" he asked. "You look as though you're deep in thought."

"Well, now that the Wolf King is dead, and the curse is broken, I'm not sure what my life's purpose is anymore."

His brows drew together in question. "What do you mean?"

"I mean, my entire life was dedicated to one single purpose—killing the Wolf King. Avenging the death of my parents.

Turns out, that wasn't even *my* purpose. It was thrust upon me by my grandmother. I'm not sure what to do with myself now."

Rowan stopped walking and turned to her, taking her hands in his. He gave them a gentle squeeze. "You'll find your purpose once again, Poppy."

She gave him a weak smile. "Do you think so?"

"I know so." He lifted one hand and kissed her palm, his lips nothing more than a brush. Even so, it sent a tingling sensation all the way up her arm. "There's an inn and tavern not far from here. What do you say we get a hot meal and a soft bed for the night?"

A broad smile erupted on her face. "That sounds wonderful."

CHAPTER 14

Rowan made good on his promise of a warm meal and a soft bed. They veered off the path as the sun dipped toward the horizon. She wondered, idly, why they didn't stay there on their way through the forest.

The Royal Ostrich was in the middle of nowhere, it seemed, off the well-traveled road surrounded by the forest. It was the only building as far as she could see and a dilapidated one at that. There seemed to be nothing royal about it, though.

"We're going to stay *here*?" she asked, trying hard to mask her disgust.

"It doesn't look like much, but it's the closest inn and the food isn't bad. One more day and we'll be back to your home village."

He waved for her to follow as he headed for the inn. She didn't have much of a choice.

"You promised me a soft bed," she reminded him.

"And you shall have it," he said with a grin.

When they entered the tavern, which was connected to the inn, there was an almost euphoric atmosphere. Every seat at the bar was filled. Every table and bench was occupied. The patrons faces were ruddy from boisterous laughter and too much ale. Barmaids balanced heavy trays laden with tankards of ale and steaming platters of food as they bustled through the room to serve the patrons.

The large, low-ceiling room was illuminated by flickering candles and the warm glow of the fire burning bright and hot in the hearth. Shadows flickered along the roughhewn walls. A bard sat on a three-legged stool by the fire, strumming a lute and singing a bawdy tale. Several in the audience sang along, clanking their tankards against each other and cheering and laughing with every chorus. On the other side of the room, a group of men played cards. Another group played a dice game throwing coins on the table with each throw. When someone won big, a loud cheer went up for the victor.

The moment Poppy smelled the tantalizing aroma of roasted meats, hearty stew, and baking bread, her stomach rumbled. While their meager rations were enough to sustain them on the hike through the forest, the last real meal they'd had was when Nana fed them before they left. The savory scents teased her senses, making her mouth water and reminding her just how long it had been since she'd tasted anything but hard bread and dried meat.

Rowan's sharp gaze swept the room, instinctively noting every exit and every unfamiliar face before his eyes settled on two empty chairs near the hearth.

"There are two seats over there."

He pointed to a table in the far corner to the left of the hearth, then headed for it. It was stuffy in the tavern as they made their way through the tables. The press of bodies made navigating the room a challenge, but no one paid them any mind, engrossed as they were in their revelry.

Amid the cacophony of laughter and song, Poppy and Rowan slipped through the tavern like shadows, unnoticed by the boisterous crowd. At the table, she removed the cloak and draped it over the back of the chair, then placed her quiver and longbow on the floor next to her.

The moment they were seated, though, a barmaid scurried over to them. Her brow was damp with sweat and her ample bosom was moments away from spilling out her tight gown. She swept a wayward lock of her wavy brown hair behind an ear.

"What can I get ye?" she asked, straining her voice over the crowd to be heard.

"A jug of mead," Rowan said, taking charge. "Loaf of bread and whatever stew you have back there. For both of us."

Nodding, she hurried off to fill their order.

Poppy missed her red cloak and the power it gave her to tap into her senses. Now more than ever she felt the loss of it, as if a piece of her was missing. She'd had the cloak all her life. Destroying it was the price for breaking the curse.

All around them, the men and women of the tavern enjoyed themselves. It almost seemed as though they were celebrating.

"They're a happy bunch," she said as her eyes darted around the room.

"You've never been to a tavern before, have you?" he asked.

"What makes you say that?"

"You're looking around in wide-eyed wonder," he said with a grin.

"Oh." She cast her eyes down and focused on the rough texture of the wood table beneath her hands, which were almost healed. "No, I haven't."

"They do seem to be overly jovial, though," he said. "I can't say I've ever been here when it was this crowded or this rowdy."

"You've been here before?"

"Many times. Sometimes, when I was in wolf form, I'd hang about the back door waiting for scraps. It was oftentimes the only meal I had that day."

There was something about the way he said it that sent a pang of sorrow through her. She wondered, then, what kind of life he had when he was cursed. A man one minute, a wolf the next. Likely, he was unable to work and live a normal life. And certainly, he'd lost his position as the royal smithy. It also made her wonder if he had any family left. Parents, siblings, a wife.

"I'm sorry you had to go through that," she said, and she meant it.

All because Nana interfered with the natural order of things. Had she left things alone, the ley lines would have erupted as they were supposed to, and the magic would have been absorbed by Damon. Perhaps things would be different. Perhaps her parents would still be alive.

Before he responded, the barmaid returned with a loaded tray. Two tankards, a jug of mead, two loaves of bread, and two steaming bowls of a thick, beef stew. She plunked it all down on the table.

"Is that all for ye?" she asked.

"What's the celebration for?" Rowan asked, motioning to the crowded tavern.

"Och, have ye no heard?" she asked.

He shook his head. "A man came earlier. Said the dire wolf terrorizing villages was dead. Saw it with his own eyes! Can ye believe it? After all these years?"

Poppy sucked in a sharp breath. Rowan, though feigned surprise.

"That is good news, to be sure."

"If there's nothin' else?" she asked, clearly impatient to get back to her duties.

"No, nothing. Thanks."

When she hurried off, Poppy asked, "Who do you suppose was the man she mentioned?"

"By my reckoning," he said, grabbing the jug and pouring two tankards of mead, "it was Louis or Frederick. One of them must have passed this way."

It made sense since they were long gone by the time she and Rowan left the temple. Poppy dug into her stew, thankful for the hot meal, while Rowan tore off a hunk of bread.

And on the morrow, she would face her Nana once again.

CHAPTER 15

The following morning, after a good night's rest, she and Rowan headed away from *The Royal Ostrich*. Another day of walking was ahead of them, but she didn't mind. She was glad to have slept in a bed instead of on the cold ground.

She continued wearing Rowan's cloak, to his insistence. He didn't even complain when the wind turned from the north though he tried to hide his shivering.

They arrived back at the edge of the village before sundown. The closer she got to the cottage she shared with Nana, the more her stomach was twisted into knots. She didn't know why she was so nervous about facing her grandmother again.

Hadn't she accomplished what she set out to do? Would Nana be happy the Wolf King was finally dead?

Poppy was unsure of her reaction.

She halted her forward motion when they were within several hundred yards of the stone cottage. Long shadows cast along the path leading to the door as the sun set in the west. Apprehension swept through her.

Rowan paused next to her, taking her hand in his.

"Everything all right?" he asked.

"Yes," she said, but she was unsure if that was the truth.

Rowan looked from her to the cottage and back again. "You know, she'll be glad to see you're back."

"I know," she said. But that wasn't what was bothering her. She turned to face him, then. "Are you coming in with me? Or is this where we say goodbye?"

The moment the words were out of her mouth, she understood her feelings. She was worried she'd never see him again. That he'd leave her here at the edge of the forest, bid her farewell, and try to return to his life.

Not only did that trouble her, but what was her life going to be now that she didn't have to avenge her parent's death? Her parents whom she had no memory of other than what Nana told her.

Their eyes met and held, the moment pounding through her. In his dark eyes, emotions swirled like storm clouds—questioning, uncertain, anguished. It mirrored the turmoil roiling within her, as if he could see the echoes of her own thoughts.

"Do you want me to come with you?" he asked, his voice tentative as if he feared her answer. "I can help tell the story."

"Yes, I'd like that." She didn't even hesitate when she said it.

The corner of his mouth lifted in a winsome smile. "Then let's go. Perhaps your Nana will feed us."

"Hungry again?" she teased. Though, in truth, her stomach rumbled at the thought of food.

While their last meal was a hearty one, it was gone after their all-day trek through the forest.

Together, they headed for the cottage, through the gate and up the cobblestone pathway. Once again, she paused at the red door, her heart pounding a wild beat as she reached for the knob. She didn't knock. Instead, she turned it and swung open the door.

Nana was sitting in her favorite chair by the hearth, an embroidery hoop in her lap, staring into the fire. When the door opened, her head snapped up, her eyes widened as she shot to her feet, the hoop forgotten. It landed on the floor at her feet. She breathed in a quiet gasp as she looked at the two of them.

"My darling girl," she said, her voice a roughened whisper.

Then she rushed across the small cottage, closing the gap between them and folding her into her embrace. Poppy wrapped her arms around her, glad to be home. Nana pulled back, holding her at arm's length. She took in her appearance. No doubt noting the missing red cloak.

"Your face is dirty. You smell like the earth and wind," she said. "I'm glad you're home." Then she took note of Rowan standing behind her. "Hello, Rowan. You made good on your promise, I see."

"Hello, Ruby."

Nana ushered them in and closed the door behind them. Poppy placed her longbow and quiver of arrows on the floor by the door. She stood a moment, relishing the cozy warmth of the cottage.

The smell of bergamot and freshly baked bread wafted from the kitchen.

"You look exhausted. Both of you. Take a seat and I'll bring tea and bread."

Nana was off to the kitchen before either of them responded. Poppy flashed him a small smile as she removed the tattered cloak from her shoulders and hung it on the peg by the door. Rowan headed for the fire, grateful, no doubt for the warmth. He stood in front of the hearth, extending his hands to warm them.

Poppy shuffled into the room and lowered herself to the chair opposite her Nana's, breathing out a heavy sigh. She hadn't realized how tired she was until she sat in that chair and let the fire warm her cold, tired bones.

Nana returned a moment later carrying a tray loaded with a teapot, cups, and a fresh loaf of brown bread. The warm yeasty smell filled the entire room as she placed the tray on the low table and poured three cups of tea. She handed one to Poppy, then Rowan, then took one for herself and sat in her chair.

They said nothing for a long moment. Poppy held the porcelain cup between her cold hands, enjoying the warmth and letting the steam rise from the tawny liquid to her face. She closed her eyes and inhaled the familiar, lovely scent.

Rowan remained standing by the fire, sipping is tea.

"Well? Are either of you going to tell me what happened?" Nana, clearly, could no longer hold her silence. "Did you find him?"

Him. The Wolf King. Damon. The man she once loved. The man she betrayed.

Poppy took a sip of the warm brew, allowing it to settle in her stomach. Then she placed the cup on the table next to the tray and busied herself with slicing the bread. It was still warm from the oven. When she had several slices, she buttered one, took her cup again, and sat back into the chair.

Rowan watched her with a curious eye as she did all this, remaining at the hearth holding his cup. His gaze darted between her and Nana, clearly wondering if she was going to answer Nana's questions. But Poppy remained mute as she sipped her tea and ate her bread.

"We found him," he finally said.

Nana's turned to him. "And?"

Rowan started to reply, but Poppy cut in. "It's a long story, Nana."

"I imagine it would be. You were gone for several days. The first night you were gone, the wolves howled all night. At first, they were far away, but as the night wore on, they came closer and closer." She sipped her tea, then looked at Rowan, her gaze hard and glinting. "Do you know anything about that?"

"Leave him be, Nana," Poppy chastised before he replied.

Nana looked somewhat taken aback at her harsh tone. Poppy took another sip of the tea.

"We were followed by his pack. They kept us safe."

"Then explain the injuries on your hands," she demanded.

"That was the Wolf King," Rowan said.

She gasped. "He attacked you?"

"He did."

"The cloak—"

"I destroyed it," she snapped.

Nana snapped her mouth shut, her jaw clenching. "It was supposed to protect you from him."

"It did for the most part," she said. She heaved a sigh then. "Nana, I think we should start at the beginning." Then she looked at him. "Don't you think so, Rowan?"

She was looking to him for any kind of moral support he wanted to give her. He nodded. "Yes, I think so."

"Then get a chair and tell me what happened," Nana demanded, her tone sharp.

"I'll get it."

Poppy popped the remaining bit of bread in her mouth and then placed her tea cup back on the low table. She went to the kitchen and brought one of the chairs from the dining table. When she was near him, he took it from her and placed it between them, his back to the fire.

When he was settled and Poppy had a refilled teacup and another piece of bread, she took her chair across from Nana. She steadied herself, letting the silence settle before she began.

An hour later, Poppy sat back in the chair, utterly exhausted. She'd told Nana the story from the day they left the cottage to when they returned. Rowan interjected his thoughts throughout the story, but for the most part, he left it to Poppy.

Nana remained seated, her hands in her lap, her lips in a thin, straight line and her sharp assessing eyes still on her.

Finally, she said, "So, it's done then. He's dead."

Anger punched Poppy at her calm words. "That's all you have to say? After everything we went through? Does it not matter to you he wanted to kill you?"

Nana rose from her seat and bent to pick up the tray. "No, Poppy. It doesn't."

There was a grim line to her lips as she lifted the tray and started to limp out of the living room. Poppy looked at Rowan whose face remained impassive. She got to her feet to follow.

"I was going to let him live," she said, the one thing she'd left out of her story.

Nana froze, her back rigid.

"I wanted to let him live," Poppy said. "To forgive him for the wrong he did to us." When her grandmother didn't move, she added, "And I do forgive him. You should, too."

Nana turned just enough to fix her with a sharp, piercing look that made Poppy's stomach twist. "Forgiveness is nothing but a hollow feeling. I will never forgive him for what he did to our family. To my village. *Never*."

Then she continued on to the kitchen.

The fire in the hearth had died. Rowan crouched and busied himself with stoking it and bringing it back to life by adding another log.

"Don't give up hope, Poppy," he said, his voice quiet so only she heard. "She may come around someday."

"Perhaps," Poppy said. "I, for one, do not wish to allow vengeance and hate to consume my life." She heaved a sigh. "What do I do now?"

"What do you mean?" he asked from his crouched position.

"My life has been about one thing—finding the Wolf King. Now that he's gone..." She paused, shook her head. "What will I do now?"

"Perhaps whatever you wish," he said.

Silence wrapped around them again. Once the fire was flaming brightly, Rowan rose to his full height.

"I should be going."

His announcement sent a pang through her. She didn't want him to leave, though she understood he had to at some point. He didn't live there with her, after all. But where did he live?

"Where will you go?"

He gave her a weak smile. "I have to find my way again."

Unsure what that meant, she got to her feet. His answer wasn't a definitive one. Though she had more questions, she said instead, "I'll walk you out."

At the door, she grabbed his tattered cloak off the peg and handed it to him. Their hands brushed. "Thank you, Rowan, for everything."

He took it from her, wrapping it around his shoulders. "I was glad to help."

Poppy opened the door and held it. Moonlight flooded the front yard in a blue-white veil. He gave her one last look, smiled, and stepped across the threshold. Unable to let him go so easily, she followed him out, closing the door behind her. The north wind gusted, lifting her hair off the back of her neck. She clutched her elbows and followed him down the path. Before he reached the gate, he halted and turned back to her.

"You do know there are ley lines that run beneath this village, don't you?"

She stared at him, her heart kicking into a wild beat as their eyes met. "There are?"

"Yes," he said.

She understood what he meant by telling her that, she thought. She clutched her elbows tighter as the wind kicked up once again.

"Will they erupt?"

Contemplation shifted over his face. "I don't know. All I do know is that if they do, there needs to be a guardian here who can take on the magic."

"And someone who can protect the village from its destruction?" she asked.

His eyes glinted. "I think someone needs to help protect the village from the destructive magic, yes."

He took a tentative step toward her.

Her heart quickened once again. It beat so hard, she thought it might beat right out of her chest. "Do you know who that someone would be?"

"Oh, I think I do." A smile tugged at the corner of his mouth.

The wind whispered through the treetops, rustling the late autumn leaves.

"Is that someone you?" she asked.

"And you, Poppy," he added. "Together, we can teach them about the magic running beneath the ground. Together, we can find a guardian to help should the time come."

Hot pinpricks of hope sprouted along the back of her neck and crawled up her scalp. Suddenly, she was lightheaded.

"Are you saying you're going to stay in the village?"

"I'd like to. If you'll have me." He reached for her hand and took it in his. "I want to stay and help you teach the villagers about the ley lines. And perhaps you'll let me help you find a new life's purpose."

Her heart pounded, each beat echoing in her ears as they locked eyes. The air between them seemed to thrum with something unspoken but undeniable. She was painfully, exquisitely aware of his touch—the way his thumb slowly, deliberately brushed across the back of her hand, sending a shiver through her whole body.

His dark eyes held hers, brimming with an emotion so deep, so raw, it stole her breath. She had seen that look once before, but now it was sharper, more intense, as though it might consume her whole. A heat bloomed in her chest, spreading like wildfire, leaving her both exhilarated and terrified of what might come next.

"I'd like that."

He squeezed her hand. "Good. There's an inn in the village. I can stay there until I can find work again."

"I know most everyone in the village. I can help you with that."

He grinned and nodded, happy to accept her offer. "We'll start tomorrow."

He kissed her, a tender brush of his lips that lingered long enough to leave her breathless. His hand released hers slowly, their fingers sliding apart as if reluctant to let go.

As he turned and headed up the path toward the gate, she stood frozen, her heart aching with the sudden emptiness where his touch had been. The soft rustle of his footsteps faded into the twilight, and she couldn't help but watch him, the way his broad shoulders moved with quiet determination.

He looked back once, his dark eyes meeting hers across the distance, carrying an intensity that sent her heart racing and left her breathless. Then he disappeared down the path toward the village square, leaving her standing there with the ghost of his kiss still warm on her lips and a longing that settled deep in her chest.

A heavy burden was lifted from her shoulders. For the first time in her life, Poppy felt as though her heart was light and unbound, free to chart her own path. No longer driven by vengeance or shaped by her grandmother's expectations, she finally understood what it meant to choose her own destiny.

Damon's death was tragic, but necessary. In his final moments, she had seen the man he once was—not a monster, but a guardian burdened by a curse he couldn't escape. A curse that changed him and turned him cold and bitter. In restoring balance, she hoped he found the peace that eluded him for so long. And maybe, someday, her grandmother would come to understand that, too.

In the distance, the howls of wolves echoed through the trees, their voices weaving through the nighttime shadows like a hymn to the past. A breeze stirred the brittle leaves, carrying away the last remnants of the forest's turmoil.

This time, Poppy listened not with fear or anticipation, but with peace and the quiet strength to face whatever came next.

Want More Magic?

Enter the Enchanted Realms where fairy tales do come true!

Once Upon a Midnight Clear, Book 1
A Christmas Cinderella Fairy Tale Retelling

A pair of enchanted glass slippers. A wicked queen. And the fate of Christmas hangs in the balance. When Ella Rose Tremaine is swept into the magical realm of Rovenheim, she must outwit a dark queen and save the Spirit of Christmas itself. Packed with romance, peril, and holiday magic, this new adventure will leave you enchanted. Available in eBook, paperback, and audiobook.

Look for the next books in the series with more coming soon!

Once Upon True Love's Kiss, Book 2
A Snow White Fairy Tale Retelling

Once Upon an Enchanted Kiss, Book 3
A Sleeping Beauty Fairy Tale Retelling

Also by Michelle Miles

Age of Wizards (Epic Fantasy)
In the Tower of the Wizard King
On the Hunt for the Wizard King

Dragon Protectors (Paranormal Shifter Romance)
Desiring the Dragon Lord
Seducing the Dragon Knight
Tempting Her Dragon Bodyguard
Dragon Protectors Book Collection (Books 1-3)

Dream Walker (Urban Fantasy)
Call of the Dark
Blood and Bone
Flame and Fury
Smoke and Ashes
Light of the World
Dream Walker Collection (Books 1-5)
Divine Heir: Dream Walker Origins

Enchanted Realms (YA Fantasy Romance)
Once Upon an Ancient Curse (Red Riding Hood)
Once Upon a Silver Strand (Rapunzel)
Once Upon a Midnight Clear (Cinderella)
Once Upon True Love's Kiss (Snow White)
Once Upon an Enchanted Kiss (Sleeping Beauty)
Once Upon an Enchanted Castle (Beauty and the Beast)

Five Towers (YA Fantasy Romance)
The Sorcerer's Daughter
Highland Destiny (Paranormal Romance) – Coming Fall 2025
Desiring the Highland Laird
Loving the Highland Warrior
Captivating the Highland Rogue

Ransom & Fortune Adventures (Time Travel Action/Adventure)
Highland Fling, Vol 1
Dead of Winter, Vol 2
The Citadel, Vol 3
Lord of the Underworld, Vol 4

Realm of Honor (Fantasy Romance)
One Knight Only

Only for a Knight

A Knight to Remember

A Knight Like No Other

Shadows of the Knight

Realm of Honor Collection (Books 1-5)

Shorts and Anthologies (Fantasy/Paranormal)

Newsletter Subscribers Only

A Dance Among the Faeries, A Short Story

Eorwulf, A Short Story

Dragons of Emhain Short Story Collection

Watch for more at MichelleMiles.net

About the Author

MICHELLE MILES believes in fairy tales, true love, and a little bit of magic in every story. She writes fantasy, paranormal, and young adult books packed with adventure, action, and swoon-worthy romance—because what's a story without a bit of danger and a whole lot of heart? From angels and demons to dragons, elves, and time travelers, her books are filled with epic quests, fierce heroines, and the kind of heroes worth falling for.

When she's not crafting new adventures, she brings stories to life as a narrator and hosts *Miles Beyond the Page*, a podcast where she chats with authors about their writing journeys. A Texas girl through and through, she loves getting lost in a good book, binge-watching movies, hiking the trails, and sipping a glass of wine. Come hang out with her on Facebook, Instagram, Pinterest, and more!

Magical Worlds, Daring Adventures, Unforgettable Romance!

Read more at MichelleMiles.net